PHILO
POTTS

OR THE HELPING HAND STRIKES AGAIN

PHILO POTTS

OR THE HELPING HAND STRIKES AGAIN

Mildred Ames

Charles Scribner's Sons   New York

To the memory of an old friend,
Hank Niemczura

Copyright © 1982 Mildred Ames

Library of Congress Cataloging in Publication Data
Ames, Mildred.
Philo Potts, or, The helping hand strikes again.
Summary: Eleven-year-old Philo and his friend
Cristabel kidnap a neighbor's neglected dog, hoping to
make his owner appreciate him, but plans go awry when
the dog makes friends with a pack of unruly strays.
[1. Dogs—Fiction.   2. Animals—Treatment—Fiction]
I. Title.   II. Title: Philo Potts.
PZ7.A5143Ph   1982   [Fic]   82-6008
ISBN 0-684-17625-4   AACR2

Contents

1

Slugger and Miss Jolly

Philo Potts loved hats. All kinds. He had so many that Poppy, his dad, made him keep most of them in the metal storage shed. "People who live in trailers shouldn't be collectors," Poppy insisted.

Philo could never resist asking, "Then how come we don't get us a house? There'd be plenty of room for everything then. We could even have a dog." And Philo *did* long for a dog.

He was silly to persist because he always got the same answer. "Takes money, Slugger—lots more than we got."

His dad often called him Slugger. That was because Philo was so big for his eleven years. And chunky. Poppy said Philo would probably be a fighter when he grew up, or maybe even a football player. He was only kidding, of course. He knew very well that Philo couldn't hurt the littlest bug, let alone another person. What's more, Philo didn't much care for the thought of getting hurt himself. So fighter was out. Nine . . . ten . . . out! So was football player.

There was another thing Philo knew he'd never be—college professor. He didn't have the brains for anything like that. Which didn't bother him at all. "There's plenty of jobs that's got to be done," Poppy always said. "Something for everybody. Why, what do you think would happen if everyone had to be a college professor? The world would stop going 'round, that's what. I tell you, Philo, there's some plumbers get more per hour than teachers. And I'll tell you something else—there's some that's worth it." And Poppy should know. He was head custodian of Jefferson Elementary School.

Philo figured that when he grew up he'd probably learn a trade, maybe even plumbing. Or maybe he'd do something really outrageous—maybe join a circus. Or, better yet, hire on at a ranch and learn how to cowboy—ride horses, round up cattle, rope those little dogies. Strange. He had lived in California all of his life and had never even seen a real ranch, didn't even know of one in the part of Los Angeles where he'd grown up.

Today, as he walked home from school, he

shifted his book bag to free a hand and run it lovingly along the brim of the straw western-style hat he wore. No wonder he'd thought of cowboying. Man, what he wouldn't give to own one of those big jobs, a real ten-gallon hat! Well, maybe someday.

Philo turned into a modest court lavishly land-scaped in concrete. A few travel trailers filled the odd spaces between mobile homes. He passed Space #4 where he lived with his dad and went on to the pink mobile home in Space #5. As he mounted the steps and rapped at the door, he could hear the television set blasting away.

"Miss Jolly," he called. "Miss Jolly."

In a moment the door opened a fraction and a bright pair of blue eyes peered suspiciously out.

"It's only me, Miss Jolly."

"Well, Lord love us! Where does the day go to? Here you are home from school already and it seems like it was lunch time only five minutes ago." She released the safety chain and opened the door on a cluttered living room where a television set seemed out of place among massive Oriental antiques.

Miss Jolly, before she'd retired, had had her own business, something she called a facial salon. As far as Philo could figure out, that was a place where mostly women went and had a lot of gook put on their faces to get what Miss Jolly said was

3

a good skin tone. Whatever that meant. She claimed she was writing a book on the subject.

The antiques were from her shop. They had given the business class, she claimed. "When you're in the beauty game," she'd told Philo, "you've got to attract rich people. They're the only ones who can afford what you're selling. And if you're going to attract rich people, you've got to have class." When she retired, she'd taken all her "class" home with her.

"Oh, these pieces still bring back the memories," she was fond of saying. "All the best people used to come to my salon. I was really somebody in those days, a real businesswoman. Supported myself, I did, and my mother. Never depended on a man, never needed one."

Miss Jolly was awfully old. Poppy said she was probably well over seventy. She had been Philo's baby-sitter for years now. Once when he was little he'd protested that he didn't need a baby-sitter. Poppy said, "You got it all wrong, Slugger. You're really sitting Miss Jolly. But we won't tell her. Okay?" Philo was still sitting Miss Jolly.

He was already taller than she. Now he drew himself up to his full height to look down on her. He noticed that she was wearing a blond hairpiece today. Above the chatter of a television commercial, he asked, "Got a new wig?"

Her frail, veiny hand rose to her head to fluff the phony hair. "How do you like it?"

"It's okay, I guess. How come you wear so many different colors?" Yesterday she'd had on a red one.

"Because," she said, giving him her you-are-really-being-very-stupid stare, "some days I want to feel fraily silver-blond and some days I want to feel fiery titian and some days I want to feel exotically brunette."

"Oh." He understood perfectly. That was exactly the way he felt about his hats. They made you feel new and different and special.

Miss Jolly hurried over to a black lacquered desk, sat on a spindly chair, donned a small pair of gold granny glasses, and stared down at a letter obviously in progress. "There are cookies out in the kitchen. Help yourself, dear. I want to finish writing to Marjorie."

"Who's that?"

She pointed to the television set. "Marjorie in 'As Life Marches On.' I know exactly how she should handle the affair between George and Susan."

5

"George and Susan?"

"George is Marjorie's husband, dear. And Susan is her childhood friend who is carrying on with George. And Marjorie doesn't seem to know what to do about it. Well, now, I had a client once who was in the same situation. She just sat her old friend down and told her a few things that only a wife could know about a husband. I tell you, that opened that brassy chit's eyes.

"That's what Marjorie should do with Susan. You know, Susan doesn't know how tight George is with money. Nor does she know that she's not the first. Oh, no. Why, just a couple of months ago he was carrying on with Jacqueline. Wait until she hears about that!"

Philo stared at her, his mouth hanging slightly open. Miss Jolly's mind was absolutely, one-hundred percent sharp and clear in every way but this. She could watch other shows with no problem, but give her a soap opera and she went flaky. She was always writing to the Marjories or the Susans to tell them how to straighten out their lives. Philo closed his mouth and shrugged. Maybe she'd give the people who wrote the shows some new ideas.

As the television commercial faded and the music for "As Life Marches On" surged forth, Philo made for the kitchen. Just as he'd thought. She'd baked her dog biscuits again. At least, that was what Poppy called them. Miss Jolly did something mysterious with cake mix that turned into these inedible lumps she called cookies, which she always seemed to have on hand. She even ate them herself. She dipped them into tea or coffee or something sickening like that. No thanks. Not for Philo. Just once, you'd think she'd have something good like peanut butter.

Philo returned to the living room. Miss Jolly was scribbling away. He said, "I don't feel much like cookies. I guess I'll go home and make myself a peanut butter sandwich."

With one eye on the television set and one eye on her letter, she said, "Be sure to lock up your place before you come back, dear."

"I won't be back till later. When I finish my sandwich, I guess I'll go out."

Now she glanced up and, over her gold glasses, gave him her conscientious-sitter stare. "Out to play?"

"No. I might go over to my cousin Todd's and fool around for a while."

As if complaining to some invisible being, she said, "In my day we went out to play. Now they fool around." She gave a mildly disapproving shake of her head. "Well, you take care, mind. And get home before your dad. You know how he worries about you."

Philo nodded. He hurried out before he could get caught up in "As Life Marches On." He thought soap operas were dumb; yet, often, he found himself watching with her, as deeply engrossed as she. Couldn't let that happen today. He had important things to do.

He made his way over to Space #4 and up the stairs of the redwood platform that served as a small porch for their trailer. He fished his wallet (a slim one that Poppy had given him for Christmas) out of his jeans pocket. Gold letters printed on it said "Genuine Leather." Every time he looked at them Philo was filled with pride. There weren't many kids he knew who had wallets, let alone one as fine as this one. In it he kept his key, a snapshot of him and Poppy, and a crisp two-dollar bill that Philo swore he'd *never, never* spend. He was convinced that two-dollar bills were rare and that someday this one would be worth a fortune.

He let himself into the trailer. "Hi," he said to the picture of his mother that sat atop the television set. "I'm home."

Sometimes he was sure he could remember his

mother when she was alive. At other times he realized that his memories were all mixed up with the stories Poppy told about her. She was a real looker, Poppy said. And she certainly *was* in that picture—just about as beautiful as anyone Philo had ever seen on television. He loved the smiling face she greeted him with every time he walked into the trailer.

He threw his book bag on the couch in the tip-out area, a section almost like a bay window that added another three feet to the width of the living area. Although he always carried a school book home, he didn't always open it.

"Man, I'm sure lucky to have a dad like Poppy," he told the picture. "Some guys come down heavy on their kids about homework. Not Poppy." The best thing about his photo-mother was she never disagreed with him. She just smiled and wished him Best Wishes in the lower corner of her picture where she'd signed her name, Joan.

He made a peanut butter sandwich, no jelly, then sprawled on the couch as he ate it, hat pushed far back on his head. Mouth full, he said "Poppy says we can't afford a house. But maybe there's a way he doesn't know about. Leastwise, I heard about this place—" He broke off. "Well, I won't say right now. I'm going to check it out today. When I'm sure, I'll let you know."

He finished his sandwich, got up, and doffed his hat to the photo the way they did it in western movies. "Adios, ma'am," he said and was off with his best cowboy swagger.

2

Cristabel Hasselbach, in Fact

Philo's trailer court fronted on Panorama Avenue, a wide boulevard. Good-sized houses along the street had once held families. Little by little people were selling the buildings to small businesses, real estate offices, beauty salons, or the like—which meant there were few children nearby. Philo had to go clear around the block to Tulip Street to find friends. He walked that way today, not because he was looking for companionship, but because that was the direction he had to take to get to his destination.

Philo liked Tulip Street. Its modest homes were, for the most part, run down, but at least they housed families rather than businesses. He liked the noise there, too, children shrieking as they played games, babies wailing, dogs barking. Amid the cacophony today he was aware of the persistent yelping of some dog in the distance.

Philo paused in front of the small apartment building where his cousin lived. He wondered if he should ask Todd to go with him. He'd have liked the company. No, he decided. Todd was too chicken. He'd never disobey his mother, Philo's Aunt Gert. "You must never go anyplace near that corridor," she'd told them more than once. "Derelicts are bound to hang out there. Gangs, too. And I hear there's packs of stray animals gone wild."

Poppy said she was as bossy as a Marine sergeant. And she sure was. Do this, don't do that! Just because she was his dad's sister she seemed to think that gave her the right to tell Philo what to do, as well as Todd. Well, it didn't! Philo was certainly glad she wasn't *his* mother. No, best to leave Todd out of this.

As Philo continued up the street, he realized he was getting closer to the yelping dog. Suddenly yelping turned into the piteous moan of an animal in trouble. Philo's eyes widened in alarm. Although plenty of kids were playing in the neighborhood, they were too absorbed in their own noise to notice anything else.

Philo hurried on until, at last, he spotted a small

dog tied to a sickly looking lemon tree that grew in the yard of a duplex. The animal had apparently circled the tree enough times to wrap the full length of its rope around it. Each time the dog strained to free itself, a choke collar tightened just a little more around its neck.

With no thought for anything but the animal, Philo wrenched open the gate of a chain-link fence and tore into the yard to struggle with the dog's collar. "No, don't tug," he chided. "You're just making it worse." In another moment, he solved the mystery of unfastening the collar and the dog was free. And none too soon, Philo decided. The poor thing could have choked to death. *Would have* if it hadn't been for Philo's quick thinking. *Philo Potts, man of action, riding on ahead of the posse today, right up front where the heroes ride.*

The dog whimpered, which Philo took as an expression of thanks. "Don't mention it," he said and again knelt to pat the animal's head and refasten its collar, safely this time.

Above him, a voice said, "I would have untangled poor Mopey myself if you hadn't come along."

Philo froze. He knew that voice. It was a voice that could cut you down to size, could ruin a whole beautiful act of heroism with a few well-chosen

13

words. He turned around and stared up at her. Cristabel Hasselbach. She was the only thing wrong with Tulip Street.

Cristabel was the kid in his class whose hand always shot up when no one else knew the answers. She was also the kid who always managed to get in the last word, and some of her last words could stretch you out pancake-flat. Philo doubted that she would have had any friends at all if her father hadn't owned Hasselbach's Bakery. Every day he gave her all the yesterday's delicacies—napoleons, éclairs, bismarcks—which, like a queen, she doled out at lunch time to those in her favor that day. Philo had never had so much as a raisin from her bounty. But who cared? Not he. He couldn't stand the girl anyhow. Didn't like her yellowy-red hair or her turned-up nose. Didn't like her freckles. If she'd had just two more on her face she'd have had a solid tan.

Philo got to his feet, pulled himself up to his full height, ran his hand along the brim of his western-style hat, and said, "One more second and I reckon that little critter there woulda been a goner."

Cristabel rolled her eyes, letting him know just what she thought of his western lingo. "Oh, no, he wouldn't. I was here almost as fast as you—right behind you, in fact. In fact, I guess I must untangle poor Mopey about a dozen times a day. In fact, I live just next door, you know."

Philo did, in fact, know very well where she lived. The Hasselbachs had the best house on the street, a big two-story structure that, Philo supposed, must have at least eight rooms. What in the world did they do with all that space? Cristabel was an only child.

Philo couldn't help drinking in the sight of the place now. What he wouldn't have given for a home like that. You could keep dogs and cats and just about anything in a place that big. He turned back to Cristabel. "You got a dog?"

"No."

"Cat?"

"No."

He shook his head. "Sure seems a shame not to have some pets in a big house like that."

"My mother says pets are too much trouble. In fact, she says they smell and their claws would scratch the hardwood floors." She sighed wistfully. "I'd sure love a dog though."

The girl liked dogs! If she liked dogs, she couldn't be all bad. Poppy always said there was some good in everybody. Philo conceded that that might, in fact, even include Cristabel, up to about one-percent's worth. He thought about all that luscious pastry from her father's shop. Maybe if you tried you could put up with the other ninety-nine percent.

Mopey was sniffing Philo's shoes now, tail wagging happily. Philo reached down to pet him. "What kind of dog is he?"

"Part basset and part something else. I don't really know, in fact."

"Who's his owner?"

"The Whipples. They both work. Somebody wanted to get rid of Mopey, so the Whipples took him to scare off burglars."

"How can he scare anybody, tied up like that?"

"They didn't always tie him up. In fact, it's only since a car went into the fence." Cristabel pointed to a section of the chain-link fence Philo hadn't noticed before, a small piece torn loose from a post but big enough to allow Mopey to escape.

"Why don't they fix it?" Philo asked.

She shrugged. "Maybe they don't know how or don't have the money to get someone else to do it. I don't know, they just don't."

Angry now, Philo said, "Man, if I had a dog, I wouldn't tie him to a tree and almost let him choke himself to death."

"I guess it's because they didn't pay anything for him, so they don't care. In fact, my dad always says that people don't value anything they don't pay for. Of course, they did spend some money for a vet. I forget the name of what Mopey had, but he was awfully sick just last week."

"He looks okay now."

"Oh, he is."

"Well, I'm not tying him back up again."

"Oh, we've *got* to."

"Not me."

"Then I'll do it. In fact, I'll tie him to the end of the porch where he can't wrap himself around anything. If we let him loose, he'll get out and get lost."

"Serve them right, those Whipples. They got no business owning a dog if they're going to treat him like that."

As Cristabel tied up the animal, Philo stomped out the gate, muttering to himself, determined to have no part in this act of cruelty. He wouldn't even watch.

He always knew there was some really good reason why he couldn't stand Cristabel Hasselbach. Now he knew what it was. She was mean. Anyone who would tie up a dog that way was, in fact, mean, mean, mean. He'd bet that in the early west she'd have been a dancehall girl, the kind you see in old westerns. Those girls were always smiling and sweet-talking all the cowboys. Just let one of those cowboys turn his back though and *pow!* Who had his pouch of gold nuggets? The dancehall girl, that's who. Oh, they were a mean bunch. No feelings. Just like Cristabel.

He had taken only a few steps when she called after him, "Where are you going?"

Surprised that she would ask, he stopped in his tracks and turned back to her. It was none of her business where he was going. He wished he could think up some really clever answer that would put her right in her place. Unfortunately, clever answers were not Philo's strong point. He thought for a moment, then looking down his nose, said, "That's for me to know and you to find out."

She giggled. "That means you're going to do something you shouldn't."

He bristled. Did she have ESP or something? "Doesn't mean any such thing." Philo scowled his meanest scowl.

She ignored it. "If you weren't going someplace you shouldn't, you wouldn't mind telling people where you were going."

He thought about that, then said, "I don't *mind* telling, I'm just *not* telling—not you or nobody else."

"You mean, *anybody* else."

He glared at her. "Don't tell me what I mean. I mean just what I said. Nobody means anybody and everybody!"

She shrugged indifferently. "If you don't want to learn English, I, in fact, couldn't care less. That's *your* problem."

"You bet it is," he sputtered. "You just, in fact, remember that!" He turned on his heel and stormed up the street. When he'd finally calmed down, he reminded himself of that good one-percent side of her. No, he still couldn't stand her. He thought again of those mouth-watering pastries and sighed. He'd just have to do without. Then he chuckled to himself. *Nobody means anybody and everybody!* He sure as shootin' got her that time. Yessir! Fastest mouth in the west.

Philo felt better. He hurried along, up Tulip Street, across Center Avenue, over to Carmalita, then straight down Vandermeer, following the directions a kid had given him. He must have walked a good fifteen minutes before he came to the highway he was looking for.

Although traffic still ran briskly along the wide road, the sidewalks looked deserted. Philo started up the street, feeling a little edgy. Where were the gangs and derelicts Aunt Gert talked about? Cars sped by him but he could see no one else around. His glance took in all the boarded-up buildings. There were not as many houses as he'd hoped for. What there were were shacky-looking places. Many foundations were still standing, so he guessed that the choice homes had already been moved.

Philo had only recently heard about what the newscaster on the five o'clock news called the forgotten corridor. Local government had condemned the area for a freeway that no one seemed to be making any attempt to build. It was a matter of economics, the newscaster said. In the meantime, people were buying up the homes and buildings cheaply and moving them to other sites. That was the part that interested Philo. He felt sure there must be a home here for him and Poppy, felt it in his stomach like an ache.

As he walked up the highway, the only sounds were the hiss of cars zooming by and the scuffing of his sneakers on the concrete sidewalk. The whole place was enough to give anyone the creeps, he thought. You felt as if you were in the middle of some strange dream. Philo didn't like this corridor. Didn't like it at all. It was a ghost town, that's what it was, and every bit as lonely and scary.

Philo turned around and made his way back the

way he had come. If there had ever been anything along that street that had been fit to live in, it was gone now. He started running, intent only on escaping from this barren section as quickly as possible.

As he was about to turn back onto the road that had taken him into the corridor, he noticed that a little farther up the highway was what looked like a wooded area. Few trees grew along the main road, so the lush greenery was a refreshing sight. Curious, he slowed to a jog and continued on toward the section. As he drew closer, he could tell that what he had taken for woods were several heavily tree-lined streets that ended at the highway. Pepper Tree Street, the sign on the nearest one said. Philo liked that. All streets should have names that nice. Surely, he thought, this part of the city couldn't be included in the condemned corridor. He decided to investigate.

Huge old pepper trees, from which the street had obviously taken its name, ran up the road as far as he could see. Late sun filtered through their droopy limbs and feathery leaves, making lacy patterns on the ground. Philo still had the eerie feeling that this was all a dream.

He soon discovered that this section, too, belonged to the corridor. All of the houses were boarded up. Yet none had been moved. Did that mean they were all for sale?

And what houses they were! There wasn't one that Philo would have refused. That is, not until he reached the end of the cul-de-sac, and there he found it—*his* house. To Philo, it looked just the way he imagined a real Spanish hacienda would look, two stories tall with white stucco walls and red tile roof. And, yes, it even had a fireplace! Philo could see all of it through a filigreed wrought-iron gate. The gate joined a concrete block wall that looked like adobe bricks and ran all around the property.

He found the latch to the gate, opened it, and went inside the yard to meet a tangle of neglected ivy. The growth threatened to swallow up a brick path leading to the front door and around to the back. Philo sauntered up the path, his eyes taking in a long front porch that he liked very much. The frustrating part of it all was that the boarded-up windows denied him a peek inside.

At the back of the house, Philo discovered a brick patio and a garden, also overgrown. A door into the building had boards nailed over what was obviously a window in it. Philo was delighted to see that someone had neglected to secure one of the boards. As he pulled it upward, the nails bent and dug into the wood. As sorry as he was to mar the door's surface, he just had to see into that house.

With the slat raised, Philo stared through dirty, cracked glass. To his disappointment, he saw only a small service area. How could he tell if this was really the house for him and Poppy when he couldn't see the rest of it?

Suddenly he had the uneasy feeling that he was not alone, that someone was watching his every move. Philo dropped the loose board, which, as he swung around, hit the door with a thud. No one anyplace. He was just jittery, he told himself, not used to quiet places with no signs of life.

Once more he went back to the door, lifted the board, and examined the cracked pane. Whoever bought the house would have to replace that window anyhow, so it wouldn't really matter if he broke in, he told himself.

Philo found that it was a simple matter to get into the service area. He merely used a rock to break the glass, then reached through and turned the doorknob. The door into the house gave him other problems. Looking through its old-fashioned keyhole, Philo decided there was a key inside. He knew very well how to cope with that problem, having watched countless old movies, but there wasn't time now. As Miss Jolly said, Poppy would worry if he was late. Better save the house for another day.

As he hurried out and headed down Pepper Tree Street, again he had the uneasy feeling that someone was watching him.

3

Spoken Like a Man

"Well, what'll it be tonight?" his dad asked Philo. "You want roast beef? Fried chicken? Turkey? Salisbury steak?" He dug farther into the refrigerator-freezer. "Now, wait a minute here. We got one more option—Mexican."

Poppy was all for options, which made everything an adventure, even eating. Most kids had to eat whatever they found on the table. His dad always saw to it that Philo had options. "I'll have Mexican," Philo said, then added quickly, "unless you want it."

"Not me. I'm in a real strong mood for a nice Salisbury steak." He took the TV dinners out of their cardboard boxes, read the directions, fixed the foil properly, and popped the food into their small oven.

"Two enchiladas, one tamale, beans, rice, and

hold the guacamole," he called to some invisible cook.

Philo laughed. He felt that he and his dad did very well in the food line, getting plenty of variety. Sometimes they had take-out food. Sometimes they even ate in restaurants. Other times they had options.

Tonight, as usual, they watched the early news on television. When their meals were ready, Poppy turned off the set. Dinner time was talk time. They settled into the cozy dining nook, foil dishes directly on the heat-proof Formica tabletop. Philo sat on one of the plastic-upholstered bench seats, his dad on the other facing him.

Philo wondered how he should lead into the subject that was uppermost in his mind. Finally he said, "Tell me about that time you and Honeybunch went horseback riding." He loved all the stories about his daredevil mother, loved his father's nickname for her. Poppy had told him the tales over and over, but Philo never tired of hearing them.

"Right now?" his dad said, sounding less enthusiastic than usual. "You've heard it about a million times."

"Yeah, but I'd like to hear it again." Philo planned to use that story to lead into his own.

"Well, okay," his dad said. "Let's see—I guess it was a Sunday in the spring."

"In March."

"Yeah, right. One Sunday in March a bunch of us guys and our dates—this was before we married, Honeybunch and me—well, we all decided to go horseback riding, me not knowing she'd never been on a horse before. We went to this stable and rented these nags."

Philo said, "And she got the old white one."

"Right. And I think to myself, at the time, this old white boy looks plenty edgy, so I speak to the guy who owns the stable. No, he says, gentle as a lamb. Says he'd put his grandmother on that horse. Well, we take his word, and I help Honeybunch up on the beast. Then I see she doesn't know one end of a horse from another."

"And you say, 'Didn't you ever ride before?' "

"Right. And she says, 'No, but there's gotta be a first time for everything.' I say to myself, 'This is some kinda date you got yourself, Potts.' Anyhow, I tell her what to do best as I can and we take off. For a while everything goes okay. We go along nice and easy, side by side. Then I don't know what happens. All of a sudden that old white horse takes off like a bat out of you-know-what and her hanging on for

27

dear life. I go galloping after and, man, I tell you I was scared."

A rapt expression on his face, Philo said, "Then that old white horse rears and she goes sliding off his back."

"Right. And I get off my horse and run over to her, afraid she's hurt bad. She lays there a minute, then she sits up and says—"

"Don't forget, you can see murder in her eyes."

"Yeah, she sits up and I see murder in her eyes. She says, 'Help me up.' I help her to her feet. I can tell she's okay. She marches over to the horse, and this old boy is standing there now, looking innocent as a newborn colt. She looks him in the eye and says, 'You damn mean four-footed devil'—only time I ever heard her swear—'I'll show you who's boss!' She gets right back up on that animal, no talking her out of it, and for the rest of the afternoon that horse is the lamb the guy says he is."

Poppy sounded finished, so Philo prompted him. "And you said—"

His dad laughed. "I said, 'Man, that's the woman for me!' "

Philo laughed, too. He loved that story, wished he could be half as brave as his mother. In every tale Poppy told about her, she was fearless. Then he re-

28

membered why he had chosen that particular story. He said now, "Speaking of four-footed animals . . ."

Poppy listened attentively as Philo related his experience with the dog that afternoon, ending with his opinion of the Whipples.

When he finished, Poppy said, "You're right, people like that don't deserve to have dogs. There oughta be a law against it. I tell you, Slugger," he jabbed his fork at Philo, "if people had to pass tests before they could have animals—or babies—this old world would not be overpopulated with the both of them."

Philo agreed.

"I'll tell you something else. People think it's their right to have a baby and their right to have an animal. In my opinion, it's not a right at all. It's a privilege!"

Again Philo agreed. He and Poppy always had their deep talks over TV dinners. Through all the heavy conversation, Philo's mother smiled and smiled at them from her spot on top of the television set.

Philo said, "I bet *I* could pass a test on how to treat a dog."

"I know you could, Philo. And it's a darn shame you can't have one. But a trailer is no place for an animal. Besides, it's against the rules here. You know that. Now, if we had us a real home, it'd be a horse of another color."

If Philo was ever going to broach the subject of the house, this was the time. "Maybe we *could* have us a home."

"Philo, I keep telling you we don't have the money."

"But maybe it wouldn't take much money." Philo went on excitedly now. "You know that place they call the forgotten corridor where they're going to put the freeway someday? There's houses there, really great houses, and they're selling them cheap. This kid in school told me his uncle bought one for practically nothing and moved it. Did you know they could move houses?"

His father sighed. "Yeah, I knew. But, Philo, there's a lot more to that kind of thing than you realize. In the first place, you gotta have a piece of land. And that costs a bundle, the price of real estate being what it is around here."

Philo wasn't about to give up so easily, but he knew better than to mention that he'd had a first-hand look at the corridor. His dad wouldn't approve any more than Aunt Gert had. "Well, maybe we could find a lot someplace where there's cheaper land."

30

"Do you realize how far we'd have to go?" His dad stared hopelessly at Philo, then answered his own question. "No, you don't. Well, believe me, by the time we found anything we could afford, we'd live so far away it would take me two days to drive to work."

"Maybe you could get another job."

"No, Philo. You don't understand. Anyplace where we could afford a lot, there wouldn't be jobs. That's the only reason why the land would be cheap in the first place. See what I mean?"

"Well, sure, but—"

"No buts. We don't have the money, pure and simple. It takes plenty to move a house, you know."

Philo eyed his Mexican dinner without appetite now.

"Look, Slugger, I know how much you want a dog. That's what you're really interested in, isn't it? It's not the house so much, is it?"

Philo nodded to the first question and shook his head to the second. True, he didn't really mind living in the trailer. But he did mind not having pets. Except for that, his life with Poppy was just perfect.

His dad waited for him to say something. When he didn't, Poppy said, "Okay. The way I see it, we got two options. First, we can rob a bank. Second, we can find me a rich woman to marry. Then we can

31

get us a great big house. You can have all the dogs you want, and I can sit around and learn how to play guitar. Did you know I always wanted to learn guitar?"

Even though Philo's Spanish hacienda was fast dissolving into the ether, he found himself smiling at the thought of his dad, who always said he had a tin ear, playing guitar. It would be a sorry day when Poppy couldn't make him smile. Philo said, "I don't like the options. I guess I better get along without a dog."

"Spoken like a man."

That was always high praise coming from Poppy. But just the same, for a while there, it had been such a lovely dream. Well, best to forget that one. Philo tried to turn his thoughts to other pleasures. "What are the options for Sunday?"

He and his dad always spent Sundays together. There were so many wonderful things to do that Poppy often came up with a long list of options— the beach, a baseball game, an exciting movie, Disneyland (Philo never tired of Disneyland), a trip to the wharf where the big ships came in and unloaded merchandise from all over the world. The choices were endless.

Or sometimes they just stayed home to watch a baseball or a football game on television. Poppy always fixed them a big bowl of popcorn and all the hot dogs the two of them could eat. Philo enjoyed those Sundays every bit as much as the others.

"The options for Sunday. . . . I'm glad you asked that question, Philo," his dad said, looking unusually serious. "I've been meaning to talk to you about—"

Philo broke in. "You got something special lined up?"

"No, wait a minute. Don't get all excited. It's not that. What I was going to say—it's—well, it's just that I've been wondering if you'd mind too much if we missed just this one Sunday?"

Mind? Of course he'd mind. That was the best day in the whole week. All the other days were only good for thinking about and looking forward to that special day. It flashed through Philo's head that once before, a long time ago, they had missed spending a Sunday together. There had been a plumbing problem at school. Poppy had spent the whole afternoon helping mop up the flood. He was very conscientious about his job. Philo said, "You got an emergency at school or something?"

Poppy seemed to shift uncomfortably in his seat. "No. Nothing like that. Well, come to think of it, it *is* kind of an emergency."

"At school?"

"No, no. Not at school. I—well, you remember that New Year's Eve party I went to?"

That was two months ago, but, yes, Philo remembered only too well. He'd had to stay with Miss Jolly, and she had accused him of being selfish, because he was mad at Poppy all that night. "New Year's Eve is a night when grown-ups want to party with other grown-ups," Miss Jolly had told him. Now he said, "Yeah, I remember."

"Remember, I told you it was at the house of this Marilyn Hotchkiss, the cashier where I take my VW for service?"

"Yeah." Philo didn't bother to try to hide the note of suspicion in his voice.

"Well, just this past week I was in the repair shop, getting my brakes adjusted, and we got to talking. She tells me how her sister-in-law that lives way up in the San Fernando Valley wants her to come up for dinner this Sunday. She doesn't mind going, she says, except that it's a long drive and she's scared to come home by herself in the dark. Then she comes right out, point-blank, and asks me if I'd mind driving her. Now, I ask you, when someone comes right out point-blank like that, what can you say?"

Philo said peevishly, "You can say no."

With a hurt look on his face, his dad said, "Aw,

come on, Philo. I taught you better than that. When someone asks you point-blank for help, you just got to do whatever you can."

"Well, why does it have to be you? Why can't she ask somebody else?"

"I don't know why. The point is, she *did* ask me, and I said I'd do it. Now, I can't very well go back on my word, can I?"

Philo said nothing.

"Aw, come on—you know I couldn't do that."

Again Philo said nothing.

"Look, it's only this once. There'll be plenty of other Sundays."

The part that really hurt was that his dad hadn't even invited him to go along, didn't want him along, he could tell. Philo scowled down into his TV dinner. "I guess I don't want any more of this stuff. It's kind of cold."

"Now look, if you're going to make such a big deal out of it—"

"I'm not making a big deal out of it—*you* are."

"You want me to tell her, no, I can't make it, my boy says I gotta stay home?"

Of course, Philo wanted him to tell her no, and one reason was as good as another. At the same time, he could well imagine the lecture Miss Jolly would hand him. "Philo, we can't always have everything our own way. We have to consider others, and we have to bend a little," she was fond of saying. If only those Sundays weren't so great, didn't mean so much to him, it would be easier. He thought it over, then said, "Go ahead and go. It's okay. After all, like you said, it's only once. We'll have plenty of other Sundays together."

Philo could sense his dad's relief, and that bothered him. Poppy smiled and reached across to give Philo a mock punch in the arm. "Spoken like a man, Slugger. Now give me that dinner and I'll stick it back in the oven. There's nothing worse than cold enchiladas."

Oh, yes, there is, Philo thought. It's a Sunday without options.

4

The Game's Afoot

"Philo, I am absolutely blitzing you," Miss Jolly said as she figured her and Philo's gin rummy scores. "You just don't seem to have your mind on the game, dear."

Which was only too true. It was Sunday-without-options day and he was feeling very sorry for himself. "Aw, who wants to play anyhow? Besides, you cheat." Normally he would never have said anything like that to her, although it *was* true. But today the only way he could deal with his own hurt was by trying to hurt someone else. It was unfair that he should suffer alone.

Miss Jolly's eyebrows inched up her forehead. "Well!" she exclaimed and nervously patted her exotically-brunette wig. "Never in all my life have I ever been accused of anything like that. Me, who's as honest as the day is long. You are no fun to play with today. No fun at all." She began gathering up the cards on the table.

Philo was sorry now. "Aw, I was just kidding."

"Besides, even if one did cheat, which of course I don't, it just isn't any fun cheating on someone whose mind isn't on the game. I must say you are in a very bad mood today. I think we'll call it quits."

Philo had to admit that Miss Jolly was right. He was in a very bad mood, and, worse, he was taking it out on her. "I'm sorry," he said. "I didn't mean to hurt your feelings. It was just a joke."

"Some joke," she said, but he thought she looked a little mollified. "What time are you supposed to go to your cousin's?"

"They don't eat until six, but I guess I might as well go over now." The time was only three o'clock, but Philo felt restless. He just didn't know what to do with himself. Poppy had arranged for him to have dinner at his cousin's because Miss Jolly always ate strange food—things like sprouts and hoop cheese, and sardines, not to mention her cake-mix dog biscuits. Aunt Gert was a good cook. "Yeah, guess I might as well go over to Todd's now. We can fool around for a while."

Miss Jolly, looking as if she was not quite up to

Philo today, said, "Good idea. And don't forget to button up your jacket. It's chilly out."

Here's your hat; what's your hurry? as Poppy would say. Well, Philo could take a hint. He'd had enough of Miss Jolly today, too. He went to the small closet off the living room and got his jacket and the deerstalker cap he'd worn. Miss Jolly never let him keep his hat on in her mobile home. Philo said, "I don't see why you won't let me wear my hat indoors."

"I've told you before, it isn't gentlemanly."

"Well, I'm not a gentleman. I'm a kid."

"But surely you want to become a gentleman someday."

Obstinately, he said, "No, I'd rather be a kid."

Miss Jolly's dark wig shook impatiently. "My, we are certainly cranky this afternoon. Get along with you. And be sure and wait at your cousin's until your dad picks you up."

Philo took off toward Todd's apartment, making his way around the block. Even Tulip Street seemed quiet and lonely today. Probably all the kids were off to fantastic places with their dads. All but Philo. He felt even more sorry for himself.

He walked absently up the street, past Todd's, and on and on aimlessly. Without even realizing it,

39

he had reached the duplex where Mopey lived. Philo stopped and stared into the yard, expecting to find it empty. But, no, there was Mopey, all wound around the lemon tree again and looking just about as miserable as Philo felt.

Right then, Philo decided to have a word with the Whipples. His fearless mother certainly wouldn't have hesitated in a case like this, and he was feeling just grumpy enough to carry it off. "Are you the owners of a badly treated dog called Mopey?" Philo would say.

"Not us," they'd say. "He just wandered into our yard and wrapped himself around the lemon tree."

Philo would be forced to look for proof. Naturally he would find it because he was wearing his deerstalker cap, the same kind of hat Sherlock Holmes always wore. Philo's keen eyes would scour their clothing. Ah, ha! From the woman's sleeve, he would lift the evidence. "Madam," he would say, "I now have proof that you are the owner of the dog, Mopey. This is one of Mopey's hairs."

"That doesn't prove anything," she'd say. "That is one of my own hairs."

"No, madam," he'd tell her, "that is not yours. You are blond. This hair is the exact color of Mopey's, reddish brown with a touch of black. Not only that, but I took something else from your sleeve." He'd hold it up to her nose. "The smell tells me this is a lemon blossom. You, madam, came away with both the hair and the blossom when you tied Mopey to the lemon tree."

Naturally she would break down and confess. Then Philo could give her and her husband a good lecture.

As he opened the gate, the clinking started Mopey barking excitedly. Philo, intent on his purpose, ignored the dog and marched right up to the front door. He rang the bell and waited. No one answered. Again he rang, but still no one answered. They were not home!

Now, there is nothing more frustrating, absolutely *nothing* more frustrating than when you're angry, really angry, and you've prepared every word of your speech, and you ring the bell and no one answers. "Okay, you Whipples," Philo growled at the door. "You asked for it." He stamped down the steps and over to Mopey. He unwound the dog and untied the rope. At least today, he noticed, Mopey was wearing an ordinary collar that couldn't choke him.

With the dog close at his feet, Philo hurried toward the fence. "Stay," he said to Mopey as he clanked out the gate and closed it behind him.

Mopey sat, head cocked, and watched Philo head up Tulip Street.

In probably no more than two seconds, just as Philo suspected, Mopey scrambled through the opening in the torn chain-link fence and started following him. Philo moved right along, pretending he didn't even see the dog. Under his breath, he murmured, "Come on, boy. We'll really give those Whipples something to worry about."

Mopey might have been Philo's dog the way his short legs waddled along beside him. He stopped every now and again to sniff out some interesting smell, then hurried to catch up. Philo, the picture of innocence, kept his eyes straight ahead. We'll take a long, long walk, he thought. In the meantime, the Whipples will surely come home. Maybe if they think they've lost Mopey, they'll start appreciating him.

Philo decided to go as far as the corridor. If a stray dog chose to follow him there, it wasn't his fault, was it? He pushed right along, up Tulip Street, across Center, over to Carmalita, and straight down Vandermeer. This time he knew exactly where he was going.

"Come on, Mopey," Philo said, "I'll show you a real neat house." He wished now that he had something to use as a leash. If a car hit the dog, it would be Philo's fault. Oh, how he'd hate himself then.

Where the busy highway met Pepper Tree Street, Philo carried Mopey across the road. The dog was a heavy burden, he found, but he couldn't take chances. On the other side, he put Mopey down and the two started up the dead-end street. At least there were no cars to worry about.

At the end of the block they entered through the wrought-iron gate into the yard of Philo's Spanish hacienda. "How about it, isn't this the greatest?" Philo said.

Mopey's rump registered approval.

Philo decided to look around the property to see if he could find something that he could use to help him get into the house. At the very back of the lot, he discovered all that remained of a small greenhouse, a structure that was little more than a shack now. Inside, Philo found all sorts of discards from the people who had once lived there. Under a broken potting bench, he spotted an old newspaper. Although soft from weather and age, he decided it would still work. Philo picked it up, then looked around until he found a rusty nail, which was perfect for pushing the key out of the lock.

Mopey, who had been frisking around the yard, joined Philo as he made for the house. At the back door, Philo lifted the loose board, then reached in to turn the knob. When the door swung open, Philo, newspaper tucked under an arm, tilted his deerstalker cap to a jauntier angle and, in a deep voice, said, "Come, Watson. The game's afoot."

Philo and Mopey had examined every room in the Spanish hacienda. Philo thought the place gloomy because of the little light that filtered through spaces in the boarded-up windows. Still, he could tell it was a nice house, with good-sized rooms as well as all kinds of interesting nooks and crannies and a really fabulous fireplace.

Entering had given him no problem. He'd merely slipped the newspaper under the door that opened into the house. Then he'd used the rusty nail to push the key out of the keyhole. When it fell on the newspaper, he'd pulled newspaper and key through to his side of the door. Simple. Nevertheless, a feat worthy of the master himself.

"Come on, Mopey," Philo said now. "I guess we've seen enough. I probably oughta take you home anyhow. We've been here for quite a while."

Mopey seemed agreeable to anything. He followed Philo out the door and waited in the service area as Philo locked up. Now the key was on the outside. He moved to turn away and leave it there, then thought better of it. He took the key and slipped it into his jacket pocket. Why did he want it? He wasn't quite sure, but, somehow, possessing the key seemed the next best thing to possessing the house.

Philo opened the outer door, and he and his deerstalker cap almost shot through the roof. He found himself staring into the nasty freckled face of Cristabel Hasselbach, who planted herself squarely in front of him.

"I knew it," she said.

Which, in fact, wasn't a surprising sentence coming from her, Philo decided. She always thought she knew everything.

Mopey greeted her happily as she said to Philo, "You're going to get into a lot of trouble for stealing the Whipples' dog. In fact, you'll probably go to jail."

"You're crazy. I didn't steal their dog. What did you do anyhow, follow us?"

"Of course not."

"Then how did you know we were here?"

"I deducted it."

Deducted? Was that the right word? Philo didn't think so. But then, what did he know about words?

When he stared at her stupidly, she said, "I fig-ured it out. Don't you know what deduction is?"

Well, of course, he knew what deduction was. Sherlock Holmes deducted all the time. "What I want to know is how you figured it out."

"I was on my way to take a present to my friend Muriel." She held up a white bakery bag, the kind she always carried her father's goodies in. "Muriel lives next door to the Whipples. I guess they'd just come home. When I passed their house they asked me if I had seen anyone in their yard. They said someone had untied Mopey and he was missing, probably stolen."

"So how'd you figure *I* had him?"

"After all you said the other day? If someone untied him, I knew it had to be you."

"But how'd you know where to find us?" As he said the words, a look of dawning spread over his face. No wonder he'd felt that someone's eyes were trained on him the day he had come here. "You followed me!"

She shrugged. "When I asked you where you were going, you said that was for you to know and me to find out. So I, in fact, found out."

"How come I never, in fact, spotted you?"

Looking very smug, she said, "*That* is for you to find out."

Man, she wasn't even wearing a deerstalker cap!

Philo said, "Well, if you want to know, I didn't steal Mopey. But I'm glad those Whipples think so. It's what I wanted them to think."

"Oh? Why?"

"Because they don't deserve a nice dog like Mopey. You just don't tie up a dog and go off and leave him all day. That's cruelty to animals."

To his surprise, she said, "They make me so mad, those people. I told them the other day that Mopey almost choked to death when they weren't there. I don't think they believed me, but they did change his collar. Then they just tied him up again." She fell silent for a time, looking as if she was turning over an idea. Finally she said, "What are you going to do about it?"

"Me? I already did it. Now I'm going to take Mopey home. Maybe they'll appreciate him more because he's been missing."

"Oh, phoo! They'll just tie him up again. In fact, there's nothing else they *can* do until that fence is fixed."

"Well, I sure can't fix the fence."

"No, but I'll bet you could make sure *they* did."

He thought he detected a crafty look in her eyes. Cautiously, he said, "How?"

"What if they couldn't have Mopey back *until* they fixed the fence?"

"You mean, me keep him? Oh, no, my dad would never go for something like that. No way."

"Well, don't tell your dad."

"Are you crazy? We live in a trailer. How you gonna hide a dog in a trailer?"

"I didn't mean you should take him home. You could leave him here until they fix the fence. Most likely it wouldn't be long once they knew they wouldn't get Mopey back until then."

Once they knew? "Who's gonna tell them—you?"

"Of course not. We'll write them a note. In fact, we can cut letters out of the newspaper and paste them on plain white paper. Then no one can ever prove who did it."

Now it was *we, us*. Philo said, "That's the same as kidnapping."

She shook her yellow-red head. "Dognapping."

He stared at her, mouth hanging open. When he could bring himself to talk, he said, "You know something? You got a real criminal mind."

"Oh, phoo! It's in a good cause, isn't it? So how can it be criminal? Besides, you were the one who wanted to help Mopey. I'm only agreeing with you. Besides, my mother says that you should always give someone in need a helping hand. That's all we'd be doing."

He wasn't too sure about her reasoning. But she was right about one thing. He did want to help Mopey. It had to be the cruelest thing in the world to tie up a dog the way the Whipples had.

Philo glanced around the overgrown yard. Not a bad place for an animal with its concrete block wall. Even the gate was dog-proof. Philo looked up at the sky. Not a cloud. On television, the weatherman had predicted a hot, dry week. No problem there. "Well, it isn't like we'd be asking for anything for ourselves, the way kidnappers always do. It would be for Mopey." As he said the words, he realized that he had, in fact, included her, this girl he couldn't stand. Well, there was no keeping her out now anyhow.

"What would we do about food?" Philo said. "I can't come back tonight with anything."

"I can't either. But these ought to hold him until tomorrow." She opened the white bag, and he could see about a half-dozen jelly doughnuts inside.

Philo wouldn't have minded having one or two himself, but of course he had to think of Mopey. "He'll sure like those. I'll bet the Whipples never give him anything that good."

They searched the former greenhouse until they found an old bucket, which they filled with water from an outdoor faucet.

Cristabel said, "Maybe you could bring him some food in the morning. I can't because my mother drives me to school."

Philo nodded. Poppy left for his job a good half-hour before Philo was off to school, so that was no problem. He was beginning to get into the spirit of this great adventure. What daring it would take. Maybe he was more like his mother than he'd thought. "We can't keep Mopey here very long though," he said firmly. "Just until after school tomorrow."

"Of course. In fact, we'll go over to my house right now and make up the letter. I have a playhouse in the back yard. We can do it there. I'll bet by tomorrow afternoon that fence will be fixed."

"It better be," Philo said.

They were partners now. Partners in crime. The game was, indeed, afoot.

5

The Helping Hand

In the morning, after breakfast, and after his dad had left, Philo made himself a peanut butter and jelly sandwich to put in his lunchbox alongside a fat dill pickle, a banana, an apple, and five chocolate chip cookies. He made a second peanut butter and jelly sandwich for Mopey. Then he put on the alpine hat Poppy had bought him at Disneyland and hurried out.

His choice of hats today had something to do with the feeling that he had risen to new heights of daring. When had he ever before taken such a chance, risked so much? If the police knew he was guilty of dognapping, he was sure he'd get years in the slammer. Yessir, he was scaling Mt. Everest. One wrong step and it was over. Philo Potts, famous mountain climber, a son worthy of his mother.

Philo headed toward the corridor, hoping the dog hadn't been too frightened or lonely. He thought about his dad, glad that things were back to normal for the two of them. Marilyn Hotchkiss and her sister-in-law had sent Philo a dozen home-made chocolate chip cookies and a big slice of pine-apple cheese cake, which helped heal his hurt a little. Not that those made up for a Sunday without Poppy. No way.

As he walked along he chuckled to himself, re-membering the note he and Cristabel had composed in her playhouse. It wasn't enough that she already had the best home on the street. Oh, no, she had to have a playhouse. And it was really something. It had two rooms, a tiny kitchen with real plumbing and a living room. Philo was sure she was spoiled rotten.

Among other things, she had a small refrigera-tor in the kitchen. Whoever heard of a kid own-ing something like that? Not Philo. "What's in the fridge?" he'd asked, envisioning éclairs and all kinds of perishable custard-filled delights. She opened the door to show him a box filled with canned soft drinks. "Oh," he said, disappointed.

"What's the matter? Don't you like pop?"

"Well, sure. Seems a shame, though, to waste

a nice fridge like that on pop. A nice fridge like that would be a good place to keep other stuff."

"What other stuff?"

"Well, I don't know. Maybe like something that would spoil if it weren't cold—maybe something like the stuff your father makes."

She made a face. "Yuk. I can't stand any of it. I give it all away."

What a weirdo! Philo had to settle for an orange soda.

They worked at her small kitchen table, clipping letters from newspapers and pasting them on the plain white paper Cristabel had taken from her father's desk. She was a good speller, which Philo was glad of because he wasn't. Of course they abbreviated where they could. When they finished, she said, "We should sign it."

"Are you crazy?"

"I don't mean with our own names—with something made up."

"How about X."

"No. Let me think."

He let her think. At length, she said, "Well, what we're doing is actually giving someone in need a helping hand, so how about signing it The Helping Hand?"

Philo shrugged. That seemed as good as anything. That out of the way, they went to work on the note, adding their official name. When they finished, the whole thing read:

WE HaVe YR dOG
we WiLL REturN hIM
WhEn YOU FiX Yr fENcE
Not beFOrE
WE meaN BuSIness
    THe hELpINg HAnD

The note had to be delivered under cover of darkness, so, to Philo's relief, Cristabel volunteered. It would be simple for her, she said, living next door. She would sneak out for a couple of minutes and slip the message through the mail drop in the Whipples' door, then run back home. In spite of the way he felt about her, Philo had to admire such courage. He had not felt the least urge to handle that job himself.

This morning, as he walked up Tulip Street, Philo took particular notice of the hole in the Whipples' fence. Still there. Of course they wouldn't have had enough time to fix it yet. They'd surely get with it this morning, though, or maybe this afternoon.

His dad had given him a Timex for Christmas,

so Philo timed himself. It took him just about fifteen minutes to get to the house on Pepper Tree Street where Mopey greeted him with frantic barking.

Philo talked baby-talk to the dog. "Was Mopey lonesome? Oh, poor boy." As he let himself in the gate, the dog jumped all over him, licking his hands, his face. Philo petted him, then gave him the peanut butter and jelly sandwich. Mopey gobbled it up in short order. Philo was almost tempted to give him the second sandwich, too, but thought better of it. He would have nothing for lunch. Besides, he had no time to waste or he'd be late for school.

"Be patient, Mopey," Philo said, patting the dog on the head. "It won't be much longer. We'll come get you after school. We'll bring some dog food, too." He glanced at his watch to discover he was very late. If he ran he could just make it. Philo dashed out the gate, hurriedly closing the dog inside. He never even looked back, because he knew what he'd see, Mopey's soulful eyes sadly following him up the street.

In the distance, Philo could hear the barking of other dogs. His Aunt Gert's fears of animals gone wild came to mind, but he put it down to his own feelings of uneasiness in the corridor. You could hear dogs barking anyplace.

✿　✿　✿

"What will we do?" Cristabel said. "The Whipples haven't fixed their fence yet."

Philo couldn't believe it. "You sure you put the note in the right place?"

"Of course I'm sure. They couldn't possibly miss it inside their door."

They'd had plenty of time, the biggest part of a day that had seemed endless to Philo. To drag things out more, after school he'd had to report in to Miss Jolly before he could meet Cristabel. They had chosen a corner on Tulip Street well beyond her house and far from his cousin's apartment. He certainly didn't want Todd in on this.

"Man, I sure am disappointed," Philo said. "I thought it would work."

"Me, too. Maybe we should send them another letter."

"Then we'd have to keep Mopey at the house another night. I don't think that's such a good idea."

"Well, let's wait and decide when we see how he's doing. I've heard that dogs don't really have any sense of time. In fact, I understand that they don't know if they've been alone a minute or an hour."

She always knew all of the answers in school, so Philo was inclined to believe her. Maybe it wouldn't hurt Mopey if they waited one more day.

56

"Well, okay," he said, "We'll decide when we see him."

Along the way they stopped at a grocery store. Between them, they managed the price of a small package of dry dog food. Then they hurried on to Pepper Tree Street. Just before they reached the Spanish hacienda he noticed something wrong. Alarmed, he said, "The gate's open!"

"It was shut tight last night. I tried it, in fact. I'll bet you didn't close it right this morning."

"Sure, I did," he said. Or was she right? He tried to remember whether or not he'd heard the click that meant the latch was in place. "Leastwise, I thought I did. I was in an awful hurry."

She said, "*I* would have made sure."

"Well, *you* weren't late for school. I *was.*" Philo glanced around. If Mopey was in the yard, surely he'd have heard them by now. "Maybe he's around back. Come on, let's look."

They searched the whole yard, but there was no sign of the dog. At one point, Philo reached up absently to shift his hat. He'd almost forgotten he'd worn the alpine, his mountain-climbing hat. Well, he was scaling Mt. Everest, all right. And he'd certainly taken that one false, careless step. Hating himself, he said, "It's no use. He's gone. And it's all my fault."

"It certainly is," she declared, not making him feel any better. "Well, we'll just have to go look for him."

"Look for him! Where?"

"I don't know where. We'll just have to pretend we're dogs. If you were a dog, where would you go?"

Philo said readily, "I'd go home."

"Well, he didn't do that or I would have known about it. I would have heard him barking."

"If I left the gate open this morning, he must have got out then." Philo asked himself, If I were a dog, where would I go? He closed his eyes and pictured himself back at the gate, closing Mopey inside the yard again. "Hey, wait a minute—I heard dogs barking someplace. If I were a dog, I'd probably go look for them."

"Where were they?"

"Way off—down the highway, I think."

"Well, I suppose we can at least look."

"Okay. Let's go. We just gotta find Mopey." Philo knew he would never forgive himself until they did.

They left Pepper Tree Street, Philo still clutching the box of dog food, and followed the highway. As they went, they glanced down each side street, calling and calling Mopey's name. Philo was only too aware of the traffic whizzing by. What if Mopey had tried to cross that busy street? He kept a sharp lookout, terrified that he might see a dog's lifeless body in the road.

Now and then they heard barking in the distance. Once they even followed the sound down a back alley behind a boarded-up shack to find a lone mutt, sniffing about among the abandoned rubble. The animal saw them, bared its teeth, and growled. They were so frightened they tore back to the highway again.

"This place is creepy," Cristabel said. "In fact, my father would be awfully mad at me if he knew I was here."

"Mine, too. As much as I hate to, maybe we'd better give up."

At that point, a sharp yapping set up someplace close by. They both stopped to listen. Cristabel pointed to what had once been a small radio and TV repair shop, according to the sign over the boarded-up entry.

"Sounds like it's coming from around back," Philo said.

"Should we take a look?"

After the last time they'd taken a look, Philo

wasn't too eager. Yet, what if it was Mopey? "I guess we better. But let's be quiet in case this is a dog like that other one."

As they tiptoed along the side of the building, again a dog started barking excitedly. Suddenly, someone gave a wild laugh. Philo and Cristabel froze.

A voice said, "Gimme the stick. I'll throw it for her."

More barking. A drunken giggle coming from someone other than the speaker. The sound of something lightweight hitting the ground, possibly a stick, and the whoosh of what must have been a dog flying after it. At the same time, the heavy aroma of some sort of smoke wafted toward them.

Cristabel wrinkled her freckled nose. Philo put a finger to his lips and beckoned her to follow. They turned around quietly and tiptoed back to the street. When they were a safe distance from the abandoned store, Philo said, "Man, we better get out of here. I just bet those guys were doing something they shouldn't."

Cristabel said, "They called the dog *her*, so it couldn't be Mopey."

They retraced their steps. Philo began to feel that every boarded-up structure held its own set of evil creatures eyeing the two of them. He walked faster, noticing that Cristabel did the same. Neither said a word. When they had nearly reached the turnoff that led away from the corridor, Cristabel grabbed Philo's arm and said, "Listen."

Again they heard barking, this time behind them. They both turned back as several dogs tore out from a side street, rounded the corner, and ran toward them. Philo couldn't have said how he knew, perhaps from their thin bodies, but he sensed immediately that this was one of the dog packs Aunt Gert had talked about. He shrank back.

Cristabel didn't seem to notice. Instead, she screamed, "Mopey! There's Mopey!"

With the sound of her voice, the whole dog pack stopped dead in its tracks and stared hostilely at them. Mopey, who was trailing the lot, stopped, too, as if he considered himself one of the pack now.

Philo had never been more frightened in his life. He eyed the large black dog that stood in front of the others, obviously their leader. The dog eyed Philo. Philo wanted to run, but he could feel Cristabel's eyes on him. Besides, if he ran, they would never get Mopey. Trying to keep the quiver out of his voice, Philo said, "Mopey, come. Come!"

Mopey wagged his tail happily and started toward them. The black dog gave a deep gutteral growl and Mopey paused. With an apologetic look

61

at Philo and Cristabel, he took his place at the rear again. Then the black dog turned quickly and bounded away from them, the others following, Mopey bringing up the rear.

"What'll we do?" Cristabel said.

Philo Potts, famous mountain climber, had no answer. He was scaling Mt. Everest and slipping, slipping, slipping. All he could do was hang on by his fingertips.

6

Oh, for a Thinking Cap

In a few seconds Philo realized he was still holding the box of dog food. What better way to lure a hungry animal? Maybe things weren't as hopeless as he'd thought. Although the pack was already well up the street, he noticed they had paused to sniff the corner of a building.

Philo said to Cristabel, "If we can just get them into the yard where we had Mopey, we'd be okay. We could keep Mopey and let them go."

"But that's impossible."

He held up the box of dog food. "Oh, no, it isn't. Not while we've got this."

"Oh, I forgot all about the food."

Which was only natural. It took a sure-footed expert to keep his wits about him when the going was rough. "Come on," he said, taking command. "We gotta get nearer."

As they hurried to close the distance between them and the dogs, Philo tore open the dog-food box. When they were only a few yards away, he took a handful of the small dry bits and threw it directly at the black dog. As a piece bounced off the animal's body, it started, then glanced sharply around to fix its gaze on Philo. Although obviously on guard, the dog snatched up one of the bits and wolfed it down. In another moment, the other dogs scrambled ravenously for the few remaining pieces.

"They sure act hungry," Philo said. He counted five dogs plus Mopey.

The animals quickly finished the food, so Philo threw a few more pieces, this time much closer to him and Cristabel. "Come on," he said to her. "We'll keep heading toward the house. It's only a couple of blocks."

"I just hope the dog food lasts that long," Cristabel said.

They moved up the highway, leaving a skimpy trail of food in their wake, but enough to keep the animals following them. When they were finally on Pepper Tree Street, Philo said, "You go ahead and open the gate." He handed her some of the food. "Put it down far enough into the yard to make sure they all go in, because Mopey's at the tail end. Then you stand outside. When they're in, we'll shut the gate." Philo Potts, famous mountain climber, was giving orders, and she, greenhorn lowlander, was taking them. He'd get them to the top of Mt. Everest yet.

The plan worked perfectly. For fear they would frighten the dogs away, they both stood well up the street and watched as the animals came to the end of Philo's food trail, then picked up on Cristabel's, which took them well into the yard. Then Philo and Cristabel quickly ran forward and slammed the gate.

"We made it," he said. The top of Mt. Everest!

In a tone that buried his great achievement under a cold, wet avalanche, she said, "I'm glad you think so."

Philo frowned. "What do you mean?"

"Well, we got Mopey in there all right. Now, how do we get him out?"

Philo hadn't thought quite that far ahead. "Well, I guess we can just call him." He shouted through the filigree work in the gate. "Here, Mopey! Come on, boy."

At the sound of his name, Mopey's tail wagged, but he made no move to separate himself from the other dogs, who were now sniffing the ground vainly for more food. The black dog gave a disdainful glance at them, then with some indiscernible signal, led the others around the house toward the back.

"Now what?" Cristabel said.

Philo didn't know. They had Mopey, but they didn't have Mopey. "You know, if we could just make friends with that black dog, we'd be okay. We could take Mopey without any problem then."

"I'm not getting anywhere near that dog. He's dangerous. In fact, we should call the SPCA. I heard on television that they're trying to round up some of the dog packs around here. Sooner or later they think they'll attack people."

It was Philo's thinking that the Society for the Prevention of Cruelty to Animals was sometimes cruel itself. He said cautiously, "What do you guess they'd do with this pack if they got them?"

"Put them to sleep, of course."

Exactly what he'd expected. "What you mean is kill them."

"Well, yes."

"Then why don't you say so?"

"Because it sounds nicer to say 'put them to sleep.' Like when someone dies you never say they died. You say they passed away. My mother says it's more refined."

As far as Philo was concerned, dead was dead.

What's more, he didn't think much of killing animals by whatever name you called it. "I'm not bringing the SPCA in on this. I wouldn't want all those deaths on *my* conscience. I'd feel like a murderer."

Cristabel said quickly, "I didn't say we *had* to call the SPCA. I just said we *should*."

"Well, right now, I figure we got enough to worry about. We gotta get Mopey out of there."

"How?"

"I don't know how. Let me think." All that came to mind was a teacher he'd had in second grade. Whenever she'd asked the class a question no one could answer, she'd say, "Now, class, let's all put on our thinking caps." At that moment Philo regretted that a thinking cap was not one of the hats among his huge collection. Finally he said, "I just can't see any other way. We just gotta make friends with that black dog."

"How?" Cristabel said again.

"The same way we got them all here—with food."

"But we're all out."

Philo glanced down at the empty box he was still clutching. "Yeah, you're right. Well, we just better get some more. You got any money?"

As it turned out, Cristabel owned a huge piggy bank that she and other members of her family had been stuffing with everything from coins to bills for as long as she could remember. "When it's full," she said, "you break it open and you're supposed to have about a thousand dollars. Of course, it's not full yet. In fact, it's probably not even half full."

"Can you break it open now?"

"Of course not. My mother would kill me."

"Then what good is it going to do us?"

"Oh, I know how to get the money out without breaking it. You just turn it upside down and put a knife in the coin slot. As you pull the knife out, something usually comes with it."

"Oh," Philo said. He had never owned a bank of any kind himself, but he had been saving for a long, long time. Although seventeen dollars was a long way from the price of the ten-gallon hat he wanted, it was a start. "Tell you what—five pounds of dog food is about two bucks. We'll go halves. I figure those guys are still starved. We'll give them a good meal and make friends at the same time."

She agreed, so they both returned home for money, then met again at the same corner of Tulip Street where they'd met earlier.

Cristabel was scowling. "Those Whipples called the police about their dog. My mother just told me."

"The police!" Although Philo had suspected

dognapping was some sort of crime, he had given little thought to encounters with police. Why couldn't the Whipples just fix their fence and have done with it? "I hope you didn't tell your mother we dognapped Mopey."

"Of course I didn't tell my mother. She'd think she had to tell the police, and then we'd both go to jail. In fact, she says they think it was kids."

Philo felt himself slipping down that mountain again. "How'd they ever guess that?"

"I just really can't imagine." Cristabel suddenly giggled. "Guess what the police told the Whipples?"

"What?"

"My mother said they told them they'd better get their fence fixed. They said little kids sometimes try to get through openings like that, and the broken metal could really rip them to pieces. Then the Whipples would be responsible."

"No kidding? What did the Whipples say about that?"

"Mrs. Whipple told my mother they'd been planning to get the fence fixed all the time. They were just waiting for insurance money from the man who hit it with his car."

Philo sneered. "I'll bet."

"Well, anyhow, Mrs. Whipple told my mother that they were going to go ahead now anyhow and fix the fence. I guess the police scared them. If some kid got hurt on it, my mother says the parents would probably sue the Whipples."

"Are the police still there?"

"My mother said they looked all around. Then they told Mrs. Whipple they'd investigate and left."

Philo said, "I guess we better get Mopey back as fast as we can. I don't want to tangle with the police."

"Me neither."

Soberly now, they made their way toward the corridor, stopping at the same grocery store they had used earlier. This time they bought a five-pound bag of dog food. Then they hurried along to the house on Pepper Tree Street.

7

A "Valorly" Deed

When Philo and Cristabel reached the house on
Pepper Tree Street, there was no sign of the dogs. As
they peered in through the gate, Cristabel said,
"Maybe they got away."

"They couldn't," Philo said. "Not with this wall
all around the house. I bet they're still around back.
We better go in and find them."

"*You* go in. I'm staying here. Those are dangerous animals. They could tear you to bits."

Philo had never before in his life been afraid of
an animal. And they had always seemed to love him.
Dogs and cats often followed him all over his neighborhood. His dad said he drew animals the way the
Pied Piper drew children. Still, these were more like
wild beasts than like people's pets. Maybe he

shouldn't chance it. Then he thought of how his mother had faced up to the horse, and he knew he had to try. Sometimes it was hard, trying to be as brave as his mother.

He said to Cristabel, "Well, if you won't help, I'll just have to do it alone."

"Go ahead. I'll wait here."

Annoyed because she wouldn't go with him, he said, "I think you're a big coward." That should get her, he thought. The words were as good as a dare.

She said, "You're right. I'm a coward."

She admitted it! That stunned him. What could you do about someone who admitted it? Nothing. Well, he was no coward. No, sir. He was Philo Potts, man of action. "Okay, then. Stay here. I'm going in!" *He'd* show her.

Philo very quietly opened the gate, stepped into the front yard, then, just as quietly, closed the gate behind him. He had a tight feeling in the pit of his stomach, realizing that he had also cut off his path of escape. Yet he couldn't take a chance on the dogs getting out of the yard. Mopey would be lost forever.

Philo walked as softly as he could along the walk. Now he wished he'd had the foresight to open the dog-food bag. If the animals charged, he could have distracted them by throwing the food. Opening it now would make noise and probably upset the pack.

He hoped Cristabel couldn't see him inching toward the back of the house. She might guess how scared he was. If only he could spot the dogs before they knew he was there. He would rip open the bag, throw some food, and pray that they would run for it and not for him.

As careful as he was trying to be, Philo suddenly stepped on something that crunched beneath his feet. Instantly, a wild chorus of barking shattered the quiet. Panic rushed through him. He could hear the dogs racing toward him, a stampede of furious animals, ready to tear him limb from limb. He shrank back against the house, unable to run, unable even to move. The food, the food! he reminded himself. With trembling fingers, he clumsily tore open the bag, plunged his hand inside, and grabbed a fistful of kibble. Before the animals could round the back corner of the house, Philo tossed the food as far beyond it as he could manage.

In another second the frenzied pack came in sight, heading toward him. He grabbed another handful of dog food and threw it far over their heads. They veered away from him and made for the food. The barking died as they chomped the pieces they found on the walk. Mopey, Philo noticed, was nosing around to ferret out whatever was lost among the weeds.

As the animals busied themselves, Philo let out a sigh of relief. He was safe for the moment. Or was he? Suddenly he was conscious of the black dog. Instead of eating, the dog watched him warily. Somewhere Philo had heard that animals can smell fear. Maybe if he could just act cool the dog wouldn't guess that he was shivering inside. Philo moved slightly away from the house. The dog's eyes never left him. Was it getting ready to spring?

"Hi, black dog," he said, trying to make his voice sound friendly and calm.

The dog eyed him hostilely.

Philo took a cautious step toward the rear of the house, a step that took him just that much closer to the animal. The dog tensed. "Hey, I'm not gonna hurt you. Honest. I like dogs." Then, sounding a bit like Cristabel, he added, "In fact, I love dogs. Especially black dogs." Somehow Philo didn't think the animal was convinced.

Philo took another tiny step. This time the dog quivered nervously, then backed away. "Hey, I'm not trying to get near you. I'm trying to go around to the patio where I can feed you guys. See, I'm just taking one little step toward the back yard. I'm not going anywhere near you. Now I'm taking another little step. I got this real great dinner in this here bag —better even than a TV dinner. You guys are really gonna love it. See, now I'm taking another little step."

Philo inched his way, step by step, around to the patio, talking constantly, explaining his every move. While the other animals milled around, hunting bits of food, paying Philo no attention, the black dog followed him. It never came closer but kept the same, safe distance away, watching suspiciously.

"See, now I'm gonna put some food down for all of you." Philo turned the bag over and shook out six neat piles of dog food. "See, I'm putting them far apart so everybody gets to eat, and no fighting." When he finished, Philo pointed to the food. "Okay, go get it."

The dog's eyes traveled over the piles on the ground, but it moved no closer. Philo said, "Oh, you want me to get out of the way? Okay. See, I'm getting back. I'll just get right out of your way. I know exactly how you feel. I don't like anybody bothering me when I eat." Philo backed slowly to the corner of the house.

When he reached it, the black dog let out a sharp yip that brought the rest of the pack flying

75

toward the patio. Immediately, one of them spotted a food pile and made for it. For a time there was a wild flurry, each dog trying to edge out another, moving from pile to pile. Finally, they all settled down and ate. Still looking uneasy, its eyes still on Philo, the black dog, too, joined them.

"Okay, I'm going," Philo said. He rounded the corner of the house and hurried back to Cristabel. Then he opened the gate and beckoned her in. "They didn't hurt me, so I don't guess they'll hurt you."

She looked reluctant although she did follow him in. "I hope you're right. I don't see what you need me for anyhow."

"It just might take two of us to get Mopey."

"I don't like this at all."

"It'll be okay." He pressed the remainder of the dog food, about a half-bag, on her.

She looked perplexed. "What do I do with this?"

"Feed the dogs, the way I did. The black dog saw me putting all that food down, so maybe he'll be more friendly with me now. If you want him to be friendly with you, you gotta put some down, too."

"Oh." She didn't look at all pleased.

Philo led her back to the patio, where the dogs were all bolting down the kibble. The black dog, instantly on guard, went rigid. "It's okay," Philo said to the animal. "I'm your friend." He pointed to Cristabel. "She's a friend, too. See, she's got food for you."

As Philo drew nearer, the animal gave a low growl. The other dogs stiffened and stopped eating. The black dog then made a strange noise, one that came from deep in its throat. In another moment the animal turned and bounded away from the patio, the other animals fast on its heels. They stood far back in the overgrown garden and eyed Philo and Cristabel.

Philo said to her, "Go ahead. Put some food out the way I did."

"What if they attack me?"

"They won't. I got it figured that they're more scared of us than we are of them."

"I hope you're right." Cristabel opened the bag and hurriedly shook out food on the little that was left of Philo's piles.

Philo called, "See, black dog, she's giving you food."

Cristabel emptied the bag. "Now what?"

"Now we get back. Then they'll come eat."

He and Cristabel moved clear to the corner of the house and waited. In a few seconds, the black

77

dog led the others back to the patio, where they all dug in again.

"How are we going to get Mopey?" Cristabel asked.

"Maybe we can sneak up and grab him now while he's eating."

"I'd be afraid. You do it."

Philo slowly moved forward, freezing anytime the black dog glanced up. Unfortunately, he was not fooling the animal. Philo got just so far before the dog let out his warning signal, and all of the animals scrambled to safety again, Mopey included.

By now, Philo had determined that the dog was a he. "It's no use," he said. "He's not going to make friends that fast."

Cristabel, sounding more sure of herself now, said, "Well, we'll just have to keep them all here another day. Sooner or later, they'll have to get used to us."

"That's what I figure. But that means we'll have to bring more food tomorrow."

"We can stop by my father's shop on the way home. He always lets me have the yesterday's."

Philo felt relieved. He hated the thought of spending all of his savings. He could just see his ten-gallon hat disappearing, a pint at a time. "I kind of hate to leave Mopey another night, but at least he'll have plenty of company. I bet by tomorrow that black dog will be so glad to see more food that we won't have a bit of trouble."

"I hope not."

As they made their way out the gate and up Tulip Street, Cristabel said, "I have to tell you— I'm really impressed. I mean, going in that yard like that, not knowing what those dogs would do."

"You went in, too."

"Yes, but I wouldn't have if you hadn't gone in first. Were you scared?"

"Me, scared?" Philo Potts, famous mountain climber, scared? "Not me."

"I was."

"Well, a lot of people would be," he said sympathetically, "but, you see, animals always take to me. If you're the kind of person animals always take to, you don't have to be scared around them. You wait, by tomorrow that black dog will be eating out of my hand."

"Well, anyhow, I'm impressed. I, in fact, would say you acted very valorly."

Philo, in fact, would have agreed with her, but he didn't know what valorly meant. "Is that a word?"

"Of course. It means brave."

"Oh." Well, you *had* to be valorly to climb a mountain like Everest.

"Something else I've been meaning to tell you —you have some really neat hats."

Philo wondered now if he could have been wrong about Cristabel Hasselbach. The girl seemed to have a pretty good head on her shoulders.

8

The Crime Becomes Official

Philo sat at the card table Miss Jolly had set up three weeks ago for the thousand-piece jigsaw puzzle her niece had given her last Christmas. "I believe she doesn't like me," Miss Jolly had complained at the time. "She never gives me a puzzle that isn't three-fourths sky. She knows I hate sky." Right now, Philo was hating sky, too. The blue pieces all looked alike to him.

Across the room, Miss Jolly relaxed on the sofa, reading the local newspaper in the light of a table lamp, one of the antiques left from her salon. Around its porcelain base dainty Oriental ladies peered out from behind fans, looking off into the distance at smoldering volcanos and graceful pagodas. Miss Jolly, small gold-rimmed glasses on the tip of her nose, was not sharing their serene view. Instead, she was intensely lost in her paper. Tonight she wore her First-Lady-look wig, which was brand-new and very expensive, she'd told Philo. Although he kept it to himself, he didn't think she looked any more like the President's wife than he did.

Philo indifferently pushed blue jigsaw pieces around the table, his mind absorbed in his own problems. He had fed the dogs leftover pastries that morning, hardly having more than a bite or two himself. Then, after school, he and Cristabel had spent more money on another five pounds of dog food. Although the animals cleaned it up, the black dog was still no friendlier than before, and Mopey still remained a part of the pack. Philo and Cristabel had again given up for the day, promising themselves they'd have another try tomorrow.

As if all that wasn't bad enough, at their evening meal his dad had to hand him yet another worry. Marilyn Hotchkiss had asked Poppy to take her to something at the Elks Club that night. Asked him point-blank. And what could you say when someone asked you point-blank?

No! No, no, no!

Well, Poppy hadn't said no. So here he was, off with Marilyn Hotchkiss again. Philo didn't like that at all. What was even worse, the woman was about to spoil another Sunday for him and Poppy.

Just because she said she'd never seen the inside of a trailer, Poppy had to say, "Come on over and see ours. Make it Sunday for dinner."

When Philo complained, Poppy said, "Well, I couldn't hardly do anything else, could I? I owe her a dinner after the nice meal I had at her sister-in-law's. We'll go to Chan's and get take-out Chinese. You like it and she said she does, too."

Who cared what she liked? Not Philo.

Miss Jolly's voice interrupted his thoughts. "For pity's sake, right in our own neighborhood. Tulip Street, no less."

Philo glanced up, not at all interested.

She read from the newspaper, "Disgruntled Dognappers Demand Doggie's Due."

Now Philo was interested. Surely they couldn't be talking about him and Cristabel.

Miss Jolly's eyes scanned the piece. "Children playing pranks, they say. Or possibly children with a grudge against those people on Tulip Street. They're not sure." She shook her First-Lady-look wig disapprovingly. "Stealing people's dogs, leaving threatening letters—"

"What dogs?"

"Actually, it was one dog. At least, that's all they know so far. Belonged to some people named Whipple."

Philo could feel the blood drain from his face. At first it had seemed as if he and Cristabel were doing a good deed. Now with the police on their trail and the story spread out before the world, it was no longer a good deed but a crime. An official crime. "What did you mean when you said one dog was all the police knew about so far?"

"You mark my words, Philo Potts, there is more to this than meets the eye. Dognappers never stop at pranks. Before you know it they want ransom. Oh, yes. Dognapping is an old, old game."

"It is?"

"It certainly is. Did you know that back in the 1800s Elizabeth Barrett's dog—Flush, I believe his name was—that was before Elizabeth married Robert Browning, the poet—she was a poet, too, you know, a lovely poet—of course, he was good, too—and, oh, what a beautiful love story theirs was—I always said if I could ever meet a man like Robert—"

"What about the dog?"

"The dog? Flush? Why, they dognapped him, of course, held him for ransom, they did, some bunch of thieves, and poor Elizabeth had to go into the worst section of London, full of cut-throats and harlots and worse, to get him back. That's what they did then, steal someone's dear pet and demand money for it."

84

"That's not like the dog in the newspaper."

"Never you mind. Not too long ago I read that the same kind of thing was going on someplace near Chicago. Now it's starting here, right in our own back yard. I think I'd just better write a letter to the editor and warn people."

Philo said, "You don't have to do that—that's not what's going on here."

"Never you mind. This is only the beginning. They start with dogs, and next it's children. No, Philo, I consider it my civic duty to write to the paper. Forewarned is forearmed, I always say."

Miss Jolly and her letters! That was all he needed. What an absolutely rotten world it was, full of dismal things like police, newspapers, Miss Jolly's letters, and Marilyn Hotchkiss. He was not feeling at all "valorly" tonight. For the rest of the evening, he stared bitterly into pieces of blue sky while Miss Jolly wrote a long, long letter.

The next morning Philo again had to take pastries to the dogs because Cristabel's mother drove her to school. He suspected that parting with her father's delicacies was a great sacrifice. Without her white bakery bags, the other kids no longer flocked about her at lunch time, he noticed.

Today Philo wore his navy blue watch cap,

which had once belonged to his dad, a leftover from the long-ago days when Poppy was in the Navy. Philo had a good reason for his choice. For one thing, the weather was nippy. He could pull the woolen hat down over his ears and feel nice and toasty. More important, this was his lucky cap. Good things often happened to him when he wore it. And he certainly needed some luck. Between unfriendly dogs and everything else, Philo Potts, old tar, was traveling in choppy seas.

This was his second morning to feed the pack. To his surprise, when he opened the gate and called, "Hi, dogs," they came bounding from behind the house almost as if they'd been waiting for him. A warning bark from their leader stopped them before they were within Philo's reach. They stood watching him, looking eager and impatient.

"Well, come on," he said and headed for the back patio, where he opened a bag that held a dozen Danish of various kinds. He had hidden it in the shed last night so that his dad wouldn't ask him about it. Philo had expected the pastries to smell musty. Instead, they smelled wonderful. He had all he could do to restrain himself from trying one. But there were two for each animal. It wouldn't be right to cheat one of the dogs out of his fair share.

Philo moved to place the pastries on the patio,

the way he had the dog food. Then a better idea struck him. Why not try something different? He grabbed a cheese Danish and held it out. "Okay, black dog," he said "if you want it, you gotta come and get it."

He could tell the animals were having a worse time holding themselves back than he was, but a growl from the leader kept them in place. Pitiful sounds issued from their throats, though. Saliva ran from their mouths. But not one moved toward Philo. Philo sighed. As hungry as they were, it was just not going to work. They were not going to disobey the black dog.

Philo was about to give up when Mopey, who was new to the pack and had probably not yet learned total obedience, broke away from the others. As fast as his short legs could carry him, he made for the cheese Danish. Instantly, the black dog was upon him, growling, nipping him away from Philo. Mopey whimpered and, without a fight, shrank back into the pack. The leader kept a disapproving eye on him until Mopey had virtually made himself invisible. Philo gave a long frustrated sigh. Lucky cap or not, it was just not going to work.

Then the black dog, apparently satisfied that Mopey knew his place now, turned back to Philo. To Philo's astonishment, the dog trotted up to him and very regally took the cheese Danish from his hand. Pastry clamped between his teeth, the animal headed for a spot on the grass a little apart from the others, then began to eat.

Well, what do you know! Philo scratched his head through his watch cap. He said, "Okay. I get it. You had to be first because you're the leader. That makes sense." While the black dog daintily nibbled on the pastry, Philo reached into the bag for another Danish and held it out toward the other dogs. "Next."

Now the dogs scrambled for it. They barked, they growled, they snapped until, finally, the most aggressive animal edged out the others and claimed its prize. Philo tried the same thing again. A second dog won the Danish this time. Each animal seemed to have its own place in the pecking order, with Mopey, naturally, at the tail end.

Philo, late again, quickly doled out the rest of the pastry, then hurried out the gate. He had almost reached school when the importance of what had happened dawned on him.

The black dog was obviously losing his fear of him. Philo believed he could have grabbed Mopey with no problem at all. Which meant that he and Cristabel could return Mopey to his home that afternoon. What a relief that would be, with no more police on their trail. Philo had the feeling that his choppy seas were calming a little. Good old watch cap. He knew when he'd put it on this morning that something good would happen. He could hardly wait to tell Cristabel.

9

Shake Hands with a Trained Dog

Philo and Cristabel had to spend more of their money on dog food that afternoon. Philo consoled himself with the thought that this would be the last time.

When they arrived at the house on Pepper Tree Street, they fed the animals first thing. Philo waited until the food disappeared before he made his move.

"Here, Mopey," Philo called to the dog. "Come on, boy."

Mopey's rump moved excitedly from side to side. He started toward Philo, then stopped, tensed, and flattened his ears, looking as if he feared another reprimand from the leader.

"Come on, Mopey," Philo said again.

When the black dog eyed them without his

usual threatening growl, Mopey inched along, almost on his stomach, toward Philo.

"He thinks he's sneaking," Cristabel said.

Philo urged the dog on until Mopey finally reached him. Then Philo knelt down and picked him up. "That's a good boy," he said. Mopey's tail wagged madly as both Philo and Cristabel petted him.

Cristabel said to Philo, "You'd better hang on to him."

Philo pointed to the dilapidated greenhouse at the rear of the property. "There's some rope in there that we can use for a leash. I'll hold Mopey if you'll go get it."

Cristabel hurried back to the structure and disappeared inside. She finally returned, and none too soon for Philo. Mopey's sturdy little body was growing heavier by the minute. Philo placed the dog on the ground. Cristabel handed him a length of rope, which he looped under the animal's collar, then tied securely in a knot. "Now we can take him home."

"Not now," Cristabel said. "Someone will see us. We'd better wait until it's dark."

Philo glanced at his watch. "Three-thirty. We'll have to wait until almost five-thirty then."

"That's all right with me. We don't eat until six."

"Me, too."

They sat on the steps that led into the service porch of the house. The dogs milled around restlessly, yet all the while with an eye on Cristabel and Philo. Philo said, "I bet that black dog will be friendly now."

"I bet he won't."

"He wouldn't have let Mopey come to us if he didn't think we were okay."

"Dogs that run in packs are vicious. Everybody knows that. I think we should open the gate and let them out."

Philo hated to think of the animals running loose again, scrounging for food in abandoned garbage pails that no longer held even garbage. He said, "I kind of like the looks of that black dog. He looks something like a Labrador retriever. I saw a program on TV once about how they use a lot of those dogs for guide dogs to lead the blind. They can't be vicious if they do that." He handed Cristabel Mopey's rope and got up. "I'm gonna see if I can make friends with him."

"You'd better be careful. He might bite."

Philo walked slowly toward the dog. He touched his watch cap once for good luck. The animal took a step backward. "Hey, I'm not going to hurt you," Philo said.

The dog regarded him uncertainly, but Philo moved steadily, carefully, forward. When he was near the animal, Philo put out his hand. "Here, you can smell me." He said to Cristabel, "He'll smell the dog food on my hands. He'll like that."

The dog stared and stared at Philo's hand. Then suddenly, as if drawing on some old memory, he lifted a paw and placed it in Philo's palm. Philo's mouth dropped open. "Hey, I think he wants to shake hands!" Philo gently pumped the dog's paw. The animal accepted the familiarity with great dignity, permitting Philo about five shakes before withdrawing its paw. Obviously, enough was enough.

To Philo's further surprise, the animal let him pat its head as its tail waved back and forth. "Man, this is a trained dog. He must have been somebody's pet."

"He's friendlier than I expected," Cristabel said.

Philo, satisfied that he had made a friend and proved that friend fit for society, once again took his place beside Cristabel on the steps. "Where do you suppose all these guys came from, anyhow?"

"I don't know. Some of them could be lost dogs, I guess. But they said on television that lots of people don't want their pets anymore, so they toss them out around here instead of taking them to the pound."

To Philo, either choice was unthinkable. "You know, if I just had a place for them, I'd take them all home myself."

"I'd be glad to take them if my mother would let me, but she won't."

Philo thought it over. "I know! We'll find them homes. There oughta be lots of people that want dogs. I bet in no time at all we'll find good homes for all of them."

Cristabel's eyes traveled over the yard where the dogs were frisking about now. "I don't know," she said doubtfully. "The pound doesn't seem to do too well finding homes for dogs."

"Yeah, but they don't have trained dogs. Didn't you see the way that black dog shook hands? People love dogs that do tricks."

"I'll bet the others aren't trained to do tricks."

"Then we'll train them. We can work with them every afternoon until we find them homes."

She seemed to like that idea. "We'd better give them names then—really special names like pedigreed dogs. Then everyone will think they're special, too."

That made sense, Philo thought. They began to plan excitedly. Cristabel was full of ideas. If they were going to keep the dogs in the yard, she insisted that each dog must have its own dish. She would borrow from the pottery in her playhouse, she said. For water, the dogs could use the same pail that had served Mopey. Next came names. The library should have tons of books with the names of pedigreed dogs, as well as books on dog care and training.

How would they look for homes? Philo had a few ideas about that. First, there was word of mouth. Telephone solicitation was another way. Leaflets delivered house to house might work. Signs in supermarkets were worth considering. Oh, there were countless ways. Everyone, just everyone, would come clamoring for their trained dogs.

When dusk fell, Philo propped open the door to the service porch of the house. "Just in case it rains," he said. "That way they'll have a dry place to sleep." Then they left the other dogs and took Mopey to sneak him back into his own yard. To Philo's relief, he saw that the Whipples' torn fence had already been patched.

"Now they won't have to tie him up anymore," Cristabel said.

Philo wished they could hang around to see Mopey's reunion with his owners, but, of course, that wasn't possible. At least, he and Cristabel could feel that they had done a good deed after all. Philo would have bet anything that the Whipples would treat their dog better from now on.

When he left Cristabel to hurry along to his trailer court, he felt so relieved. They would no longer have to worry about the police. And working with the dogs, for whatever short time they had them, would be almost like having dogs of their own. Of course, he would probably go through the fifteen dollars he had remaining, but he just had to tell himself that what he was doing for those animals was worth a sacrifice that big.

Yessir, he was sure glad he'd worn his watch cap today. Philo Potts, old tar, had weathered quite a squall. From now on, it was smooth sailing. Then he thought of Marilyn Hotchkiss. Squall behind. Typhoon ahead.

"Well, I just think this is plumb cozy," Marilyn Hotchkiss said, her eyes sweeping around the trailer that Philo and his dad had worked all Sunday morning to clean. Now Poppy had gone for take-out food, leaving Philo all alone with Marilyn. She talked funny, he thought. Poppy said she was a former Texan. Maybe that was why.

"Is that your mama, honey?" she said, pointing to the photograph on the television set.

Philo nodded.

"Why, she's just about as pretty as a movie star."

96

Again Philo nodded. He thought Marilyn wasn't at all pretty.

She glanced around. "Where do y'all bed down?"

Philo pointed to the small bathroom that separated the living area from the sleeping area. "Through there."

"Mind if I have a look-see?"

Philo shook his head.

Marilyn opened the sliding door that led into the bathroom, then the door that opened into the tiny room where Philo and his dad had their usually unmade bunk beds. Today, as Poppy put it, everything was ship-shape.

While she was examining that part of the trailer, Philo's thoughts turned to the dogs. He wondered if Cristabel had fed them and spent time with them as she'd promised. He knew she wasn't fond of going alone to the corridor, but there was nothing he could do about it today without making Poppy suspicious.

How Poppy had laughed when he saw Miss Jolly's long letter in the newspaper, a letter that predicted a siege of dognapping. In the same paper, a small article mentioned that "Devious Dognappers Return Dog." Although he was glad he went unnamed Philo felt just a little bit famous.

The dogs were getting more and more used to him and Cristabel, yet Philo hadn't managed to teach them one trick. Cristabel maintained that they must go to the library and get books on the subject, but somehow neither had found the time so far. Tomorrow, for sure, they'd go. And they should start putting up signs in supermarkets, too. In the meantime, the dogs were fast eating up his money.

As Marilyn returned to the living area and seated herself on the couch in the tip-out section, he put the animals out of his mind.

Marilyn said, "Well, you can't hardly say y'all have much in the way of elbow space, can you?"

Her "can't" sounded more like "cain't" to Philo.

"But it's sure cozy," she said again. "I'll just bet you sleep in the top bunk."

How did she guess that? Again Philo merely nodded. He tried to look her over without being too obvious. She wore jeans and a red turtleneck sweater. Her brown eyes darted around the room in a way that made him feel she could see the dirt he'd swept under the mat by the sink that morning. Although her hair was mostly dark, it was shot with gray. She was probably awfully old, he decided.

As if she had read his mind, she said, "How old are you, honey?"

"Eleven. How old are you?"

She laughed. "Ordinarily I don't tell just anybody my age, but I'll tell you. I'm thirty-two."

He knew it! She was really old. You'd think somebody that age would be married. "You got a husband?"

"Not anymore."

What did that mean? Thinking of his mother, Philo said, "Is he dead?"

"Oh, my stars, no! We divorced years ago. He got the car and I got the mortgage on the house."

Philo persisted. "How come you got divorced?"

For a moment she looked at a loss. "Well, I guess we just didn't like livin' together anymore."

"Why?"

"Why? There just isn't any *why* to things like that. We didn't get along. That's about all I can tell you, honey. When folks don't get along, it's better if they split up. Y'understand?"

Philo understood, all right. Her husband divorced her because he didn't like living with her, couldn't get along with her. Most likely nobody could. Then an interesting idea struck him. "Did you say you had a house?"

"Yes, I did—a nice little three-bedroom tract house in Laurel Knolls. I was lucky—bought it before the prices went clear out of sight around here."

"You got a dog?"

She smiled. "Not since my sweet Phoebe-Ethel died. I just knew I'd never find another dog like her."

She'd called the dog sweet, so most likely the dog had gotten along with Marilyn even though her husband hadn't. "You got a fenced yard?"

"My stars! You're just full of questions, now, aren't you? Yes, I got a fenced yard. I had to put one in for Phoebe-Ethel."

That was all Philo wanted to know. If worse came to worse, she would make a possible candidate for dog adoption. She had one big strike against her, though—she worked.

"Y'all like chili—you and your daddy?" Marilyn asked.

"Sure," Philo said without thinking.

"Then you'll have to bring your daddy over to my house some night real soon. I make the best Texas Panhandle chili you ever tasted in your life."

Now he wished he'd said he hated chili. On second thought, though, it was probably a good idea to go to her house. That way he could see with his own eyes if her home was the kind he'd let one of his trained dogs go to. You couldn't be too fussy about something like that.

Poppy finally came home with carton after carton of Chinese food, more variety than the two of

100

them ever bought when they were alone. After they all finished eating, there was still enough left over for Monday's dinner.

For the rest of the evening they watched a movie on television, then Poppy drove Marilyn home. When he came back, Philo was still watching television.

"Well, what do you think of Marilyn?" Poppy said.

Philo took his eyes from the picture and shrugged. "She's okay, I guess. How come she says 'cain't'?"

"That's the way they talk in Texas."

"Did you know she's divorced?"

"Sure I knew."

"You know why?"

Poppy looked puzzled. "Why?"

"Because her husband didn't like living with her. He couldn't get along with her. I guess maybe she's just hard to get along with."

Poppy said very seriously, "That bad, huh?"

Just as seriously, Philo nodded. "Well, one thing I'll say for her, she liked her dog."

Although Philo could see nothing funny, Poppy started laughing. When he stopped he said, "Well, I always say there's gotta be a little good in everybody."

10 ❧

Pepper Tree Acres, Home of Champions

The following week was a busy one for Philo and Cristabel. They borrowed an encyclopedia on dogs from the library, as well as a dog training and care book, and set about the task of getting the animals ready for adoption.

Cristabel was very systematic. She kept a small card for each dog. "We'll put name, sex, breed, and remarks on these. Then we won't forget what we decided," she said.

"What remarks?" Philo asked.

"Oh, like 'good with small children'—remarks like that."

"How are we gonna find that out?"

"We'll guess."

"How about breed—we gonna guess that, too?"

"Of course. The encyclopedia is full of pictures. We just have to decide which breeds look like our dogs."

To Philo and Cristabel, they were now "our" dogs. From the library books, Cristabel learned that pedigreed dogs often came from important-sounding kennels. She insisted they must first find a good name for *their* operation. Philo suggested they use the name of the street, Pepper Tree. No, the kennels in the books were mostly called Something-or-Other Acres, Cristabel maintained. Then theirs would have "Acres," too, Pepper Tree Acres. A perfect name for a distinguished kennel, a home of champions.

Now to name the dogs. The pictures in the encyclopedia told them that the black dog looked something like a Labrador retriever and something like a Doberman pinscher. He became:

Rajah, Royal Ruler of Pepper Tree Acres
Sex: Male
Breed: Labrador pinscher
Remarks: One of a kind. A jewel among dogs.

There were two females in the pack. One was white, red, and dark brown. She became Princess Starlight of Pepper Tree Acres, a dachshund Beagle.

The second, the plumpest of all the dogs, was pure Irish terrier, Philo and Cristabel were sure. They named her Emerald.

Of the two remaining males, one had the flat face of a bull, the other a long collie-like muzzle. The bull-face became Maximillian (a name Cristabel said came right out of royalty). The other they called Prince Charles. And all, of course, were "of Pepper Tree Acres."

Now that the animals were properly named and catalogued, the fun was over and the work beginning. Philo had never dreamed that dogs required all the care the library books recommended. For one thing, they needed regular grooming, which meant laying out money for a brush. Fortunately, the animals were friendly now and thoroughly enjoyed all the attention. Although Philo and Cristabel took turns, Philo always managed to brush his favorite, Rajah, Royal Ruler of Pepper Tree Acres.

In addition to the brush, they had to put out more money for cheap collars for each of the dogs as well as one leash. The leash, Philo discovered from one of the books, was necessary for training. He also discovered that he had been doing everything wrong.

When the books talked about training, he was

disappointed to find out, they meant obedience training. "They don't even tell you how to get a dog to roll over and play dead," he said to Cristabel.

"I guess people would rather have their dogs learn how to mind," she said.

It was just as well, Philo decided. He and Cristabel would have enough trouble teaching all the dogs to sit, stay, heel, come, and everything else it took to produce a well-behaved animal. And he was right. With the single leash, they could work with only one dog at a time. The job was frustrating, too. Rajah and Princess Starlight were eager to please, but the others seemed completely indifferent. They yawned and did everything but what they were told.

Philo and Cristabel also learned from the books that pastries were improper food for dogs. That seemed to please Cristabel. She was only too happy to keep all her "yesterday's" to win back her fair-weather friends, Philo suspected. He still continued to visit the dogs in the morning, though. Now he brought dog biscuits. Oh, he and Cristabel were learning, all right, but everything they learned seemed to mean more money.

Naturally, the dogs needed exercise, too. When Philo and Cristabel weren't trying to train them, they tossed sticks for the animals or played games with them—anything to get them running around the yard. Taking them outside into the corridor held too many hazards.

And then there was the cleanup, something Philo hadn't even bargained for. The five dogs left messes wherever it suited them. Cristabel found a rusted trowel in the greenhouse. They took turns scooping up dog droppings from the patio, depositing them in a paper bag, then in a low area in the far back corner of the yard like a compost pile. All in all, the dogs took up every free moment of their time.

Cristabel had to spread the word around school that several wonderful dogs were available for adoption. "If I do it," Philo told her, "my cousin Todd will know something's going on. I sure don't want him in on the deal." So far, her efforts were to no avail, so they composed a notice for the supermarket bulletin boards in their neighborhood.

> Dog Lovers, Do You Have A Fenced Yard? Pepper Tree Acres, Kennel Of Champions, Will Part With A Few Trained Dogs. To Good Homes Only. No Others Need Apply. We Are Fussy.

They listed Cristabel's phone number. Cristabel said, "I'll tell my parents that one of my friends has to get rid of some dogs because she has a sick grandmother at home. In fact, I can even say they had to disconnect their phone because the grandmother couldn't be disturbed. That's why I said she could use mine."

Philo had to admire what he thought of as Cristabel's criminal mind. She was always ready with a lie to cover every guilt-ridden situation. "Good idea," he said, but he wasn't sure he'd care to tell Poppy the same thing.

On Thursday morning Philo, as usual, stopped by the yard to give the dogs the biscuits he now stored inside the house. He was thinking about Marilyn Hotchkiss. He and Poppy were going to her house that night for chili and, more important, for Philo to look over the yard and decide whether she was worthy of owning one of his trained dogs. As the dogs came to greet him now, he wondered which one he might offer her. Emerald, probably. Marilyn had had a female before, so she'd probably want another.

Philo noticed now that Emerald was not among the other dogs. He took a hurried look around the yard but couldn't find her. Worried, he glanced into the service area of the house, hoping she had gone off by herself to sleep. No, the small room was empty. What could have happened to her? There was no way she could have escaped. Was she lying sick someplace? Dead? He began to feel panicky.

Philo checked the yard again, the dogs trailing after him. This time he looked behind the old greenhouse, a spot he had missed before. Still no sign of her. He glanced inside the shacky structure but saw nothing that wasn't there before. He was about to turn away when he heard strange noises. The sounds seemed to come from behind an old, three-legged, overturned potting table. As Philo walked cautiously toward it, he heard a soft warning growl.

Although he was afraid of what he would find, he made himself peer around behind the broken table. Yes, he was right. Emerald lay on her side on an old burlap sack on the ground, not even getting to her feet when she saw him. Instead, she glanced up nervously. Then he saw why. A bunch of tiny, squirming bodies, hardly recognizable as puppies, busily suckled their mother.

Philo counted them. Five. He stared and stared at them in wonder. His eyes moistened with the pleasure the unexpected find gave him. Oh, it was beautiful—the most beautiful sight he had ever seen. Although he wanted to pick up a puppy and cuddle it, he didn't dare. He sensed that he would only upset Emerald if he drew closer, so he left dog biscuits near her chosen nest, fed the other animals, then went on to school.

He could hardly wait to tell Cristabel, yet he was glad he'd been there first to see Emerald and her puppies, glad he'd been alone. If he had shared the sight with anyone else, it wouldn't have been the same experience at all. Then the sad truth struck him. Instead of homes for five dogs, they now had to find homes for ten. Wow!

By the time Philo and his dad headed for Marilyn's house, Philo felt as if he'd had a very full day. He and Cristabel had spent all afternoon with the dogs, grooming them, trying to train them, cleaning up messes, playing with them, and taking about a million peeks at the new puppies. They didn't touch the pups, though. Emerald growled if even a curious dog came too close.

Tonight Philo wore what he thought of as his auto-racing cap. He had bought it at a foreign car show he'd gone to with Poppy on one of their special Sundays. One of the booths had shown a movie of an exciting race at someplace called Le Mans in France, a race won by a Porsche racing car. That was why Philo had to have this particular cap. It was white with the bold black letters PORSCHE across the peak. An inset of black and white checks ran like a ribbon from front center to back, suggesting the checkered flag that signaled the winner of the race. Tonight, of course, Philo was merely on a test run.

Although it was almost dark he could see that trees lined Marilyn's street. One point for her. Dogs liked trees. Poppy pulled the Volkswagon into a driveway and parked in front of a two-car garage. Philo took in a light-colored stucco bungalow with a tree in the middle of a small lawn. Another tree, another point for Marilyn. And, yes, there it was— the porch light shone on a sturdy, concrete-block wall, separating her house from the neighbor's. A good ten points right there.

As they strode up the walk, the front door swung open and Marilyn appeared. "Hi," she said, "I been watchin' for you. Y'all come on in."

She led them through a small hall and into a living-dining room with big windows that looked out onto a lighted patio. Beyond the patio, a lawn stretched into a good-sized yard. A fine place for a dog.

Philo said, "That would make a neat yard for a dog."

Poppy chuckled. "That's all this guy ever thinks about. Long as I can remember he's wanted a dog."

"Too bad you can't have one in a trailer," Marilyn said sympathetically.

Philo nodded toward the window. "That's because we don't have a nice yard like that. If we had a nice yard like that, we'd sure have a dog. Wouldn't we, Poppy?"

"Sure," his dad said.

Philo persisted. "Anyone with a nice yard like that oughta have a dog."

"Hey, now, don't you go telling Marilyn what she oughta have. If she wanted a dog, she'd get one."

"Dogs take lots of lookin' after, honey. And they're destructive. My sweet Phoebe-Ethel had the whole back yard dug up. My stars, it was a sight, not a blade of grass anywhere." She stared out the big windows as if still seeing a wasteland.

Minus a couple of points there. She didn't like her yard dug up.

Marilyn turned back to the two of them. "I'll bet y'all are just about as hungry as a woodpecker with a headache."

Poppy howled. Philo couldn't see anything funny about a woodpecker with a headache.

"Just sit down and make yourselves to home.

Everythin's all ready." She gestured toward the table in the dining portion of the room.

Philo noticed that she had already laid out dishes and flatware. A crisp white-and-red-checked tablecloth covered the table. That meant he'd have to be extra careful. Aunt Gert used a tablecloth only at Christmas. If you got so much as a drop of gravy on it, she'd yell her head off, call you a slob with no manners and everything else. That reminded Philo. He took off his cap the way Miss Jolly had taught him and placed it on an end table in the living room. He didn't think he'd enjoy this meal very much.

He was wrong. Everything was delicious: the green salad with avocado dressing, her homemade chili, fresh-baked biscuits, a frozen dessert that tasted chocolate and mint at the same time, and big, soft, cake-like cookies. There was milk for him and beer for Poppy. And she didn't even raise an eyebrow when a drop of his chocolate dessert soaked into the tablecloth like a spot of ink.

When he apologized, she said, "Don't you worry your head none about a li'l ole nothin' like that, honey. It'll wash right out."

After dinner Philo watched television in a small room she called "the den" while Poppy and Marilyn talked and laughed in the living room. Philo thought he'd never heard his dad laugh so much. After the cramped trailer, Marilyn's house seemed enormous to Philo. He wondered how it would feel to live in a place that big, a place with a room—no, a den— just for watching television. Of course, it wasn't as big as the Pepper Tree Street house, but it was nice. It would make a good home for one of his dogs.

When Poppy finally said it was time to leave, Philo retrieved his cap from the living room and joined Marilyn and his dad, who were already at the front door.

As Marilyn moved to open it, Poppy said, "Marilyn, you oughta have a bolt on that door. A lock like you got there would be a cinch for a burglar to open. You know, you can't be too careful these days."

"I know you're right," Marilyn said. "I been fixin' to do somethin' about it. Just haven't got to it yet."

Poppy said, "I'll get you one tomorrow. How about if I stop by tomorrow night and put it on?"

"Oh, I hate to put you to all that trouble, but I'd sure appreciate it if you would."

"No trouble," Poppy said.

Philo didn't much care for the way the conversation was going. He put on his auto-racing cap. As he listened to the discussion about locks, he suddenly thought of a brilliant solution to Marilyn's

problem. Varoom! Coming right down the straight-
away, checkered flag plainly in sight. Philo said,
"What you really need is a good watch dog."

Both Marilyn and Poppy looked at Philo,
looked at each other, then they both broke up.

Philo saw nothing funny.

When Poppy stopped laughing, he took out his
car keys and handed them to Philo. "Here. You go
ahead and open the car. I'll be right along. I want
another look at this door before I decide what kind
of lock to get."

Philo sullenly started down the walk.

Marilyn called after him, "Y'all hurry back,
honey."

Then the door closed, no doubt for Poppy to
do what he planned to do. And Philo thought he
knew just what that was. He was willing to give one
of his dogs to Marilyn but not his dad.

11

Panorama Animal Hospital

After school the next day Philo checked in with Miss Jolly. He would have asked her to take one of his dogs, but she had told him many times that she didn't want one. She was afraid that, at her age, the animal would outlive her and no one else would want it. Instead, he told her all about the previous evening with Marilyn. "The next thing you know, he'll be marrying her," he said.

He had voiced the same opinion to his dad on the ride home last night. Poppy said good-naturedly, "Now don't go putting ideas in my head."

"You mean you *would?*" Philo asked.

"Come on now. I'm not marrying anybody— leastwise, not without you having a say in the matter."

"I'd say no. I don't even know why you like her."

"Why I like her—Come to think of it, I *do* like Marilyn. I guess it's because she makes me laugh so much. You know, Slugger, it's a comfortable thing to be around someone who makes you laugh."

"I guess I could think up ways to make you laugh, too."

"Sure you could. You already do. And don't you go worrying about me marrying Marilyn. She'd never have me."

Then she had to be crazy, Philo thought, but he didn't say it. Poppy had immediately changed the subject. "What do you say we go camping on Easter vacation? That's not too far away now."

Philo immediately thought of his dogs. Oh, well, they'd all have homes by that time. "That would be great." Then he added suspiciously, "Just us?"

"Well, sure, just us."

Great. Marilyn couldn't be too important then. Camping made Philo think of his mother. "That reminds me of the time you and Honeybunch went camping in the desert." Poppy had gone on ahead that day, hiking along the trail up a steep mountain. The earth had given way beneath his feet and taken him with it all the way to the bottom of a deep canyon. When he tried to pick himself up, he realized his leg was broken. If it hadn't been for Honeybunch, he'd told Philo many times, he would have died. She took their car and drove miles and miles before she found help. Philo loved that story. It could have been a suspense movie on television the way Poppy always told it. In his head, Philo had even given it a title: The Narrow Escape. To get his dad started, he said, "That sure was a narrow escape you had."

"Yeah, sure was."

"Tell me about it again. I forget some of it."

"Slugger, you know that story better than I do."

"But I like to hear you tell it."

"Not tonight, huh?" As he pulled into their trailer court he'd said, "How about that—can't be more than five minutes portal to portal from Marilyn's place to ours."

So much for Honeybunch. Philo hadn't liked that at all.

Miss Jolly, a blond today, listened to Philo's account of the evening as she worked on the hateful blue sky pieces of her jigsaw puzzle. Somehow he didn't quite feel she was taking in the seriousness of the situation. He said, "Maybe I should just tell her to leave the both of us alone, Poppy and me."

Miss Jolly's delicately penciled brows shot up.

"Philo Potts, you just stay out of it! I saw the same thing happen on 'Life's Children' on television. Sandra, who was twelve and should have known better—I wrote and told her so—wouldn't let her dad marry Kathleen, a first-rate nurse, mind you, not some trollop, a perfectly lovely woman and the true love of his life. It broke his heart and Kathleen's, too. Oh, no, Philo. You mustn't tamper with other people's lives."

"What about *my* life?"

"Philo, in no time at all you'll be grown up and leaving your dad to go out on your own."

"Not for years and years. Maybe never."

"In any case, your dad is a grown man and he needs friends his own age, just the way you do."

"But not a girlfriend."

"Why not a girlfriend? Or even a wife? People need love."

"Well, I love him, don't I?"

"Of course you do, dear. But that's not quite the same thing. A man wants a woman to love, too."

"But she's ugly. Man, my mother was a hundred times prettier."

Miss Jolly became suddenly absorbed in fitting pieces of her puzzle together. She did not look up as she said, "Pretty isn't everything. Besides, you tend to exaggerate, Philo. You don't even remember your mother."

"Maybe not, but I've got her picture. I can see."

Miss Jolly was thoughtful for a moment. Then she said, "Pictures sometimes lie."

"What do you mean—lie?"

She began fooling with the blond wig, the way she sometimes did when she was flustered. Finally she said, "I mean, pictures sometimes flatter people. Your mother probably wasn't quite as pretty as that picture, any more than Marilyn is as ugly as you make out. In fact, she's not ugly at all. I got a peek at her the day she was visiting you. I like her looks. She has a nice honest face—very good skin. Of course, she's a little on the thin side, but she'll live longer that way."

Well, maybe he did exaggerate a little. But only a little. He hated for Miss Jolly to think he was being deliberately mean, so he said, "Well, one thing I'll say for her, she's a good cook."

"Exactly what you and your dad need. You eat far too many TV dinners and too much take-out food. Full of salt and sugar and fat, all that stuff is. You'll have high blood pressure before you're fifty years old."

That gave him a whole half-century to enjoy

hamburgers, hot dogs, milk shakes, pizza, fried chicken, and the like. He might even be sick of them by then. At any rate, he couldn't trouble himself about something that far away. He had more immediate worries, ten dogs waiting anxiously for food and good homes.

Philo had told Cristabel he would meet her at the Pepper Tree Street house that afternoon. He wore his baseball cap, but all it did for him was remind him that there would be no time for games of any kind until he and Cristabel had placed their dogs. Also, his money was running short. Cristabel said she still had plenty in that big pig of hers. Still, it didn't seem fair to let her pay more than he did.

As he let himself in the gate, the dogs bounded toward him, all of them vying for his attention. Then Cristabel appeared from someplace. From the distressed look on her face, Philo knew something was wrong.

"Oh, poor Emerald," she said. "Two of her puppies are dead."

Philo couldn't believe her. "What do you mean, dead? They were all okay this morning."

"Well, they're not now. Maybe they were sick and we just didn't realize it."

Philo felt a little sick himself. "What did you do with them?"

"I scooped them up with that old trowel we use to clean up. Emerald didn't even growl at me. I found a box in the shack and put them in it. We'll have to bury them."

"You sure they're dead?"

"Of course, I'm sure. They're icy cold."

"How'd you know that?"

"I felt them."

Philo could never have brought himself to do something like that. "Is Emerald okay?"

"She's nursing the other pups. I don't think she even realizes."

Grimly, they took turns working with the trowel, digging behind the old greenhouse where the earth was soft, until they had a hole big enough for the box with the tiny bodies. Although Philo felt sad, he hadn't known the pups long enough to miss them. He felt almost guilty when it ran through his head that there were two fewer homes he and Cristabel would have to find.

The following day was Saturday. Poppy had a plumbing emergency at school, a flood that he said would tie him up all day. After he left their trailer, Philo phoned Cristabel, and a short time later they met at their customary spot on Tulip Street, to

121

hurry along to the corridor. Philo planned to spend most of the day with the dogs. Cristabel's mother wanted her home by late morning to take her shopping.

As usual, the dogs, barking excitedly, met them at the gate and followed them back to the patio. Philo stored the food in the kitchen now, just off the service porch, where the dogs couldn't get at it. To get in, he had to use the key he constantly carried in his pocket.

The key was now as necessary to his daily dress as his hats. He loved the feel of it in his hand, loved to put it in the lock, turn it smartly, then open the door that led into *his* house. At least, that was the way he thought of the place. Cristabel wanted no part of it. She wouldn't even explore it with him. The only time she had peeked in, she'd declared it creepy and spooky. Of course, Cristabel already had a perfectly fine house of her own.

While he was getting the dog biscuits, she had gone directly to the shack to check on the new family. Philo was giving each animal its morning snack when he saw her running toward him, a stricken expression on her face.

"Oh, it's awful," she said. "The pups are all dead. And Emerald—Oh, come quick."

Philo was so stunned he thought he'd surely

heard wrong. Yet he couldn't bring himself to ask her to repeat the words. He set the box of dog biscuits on the patio and rushed after her into the shack, his stomach as tight as a clenched fist.

She led him back to the overturned potting table. He could hardly force himself to look behind it, but he did. No, he hadn't heard wrong. All three pups lay still, lifeless, looking like lumps of clay. Emerald sprawled close by, her breathing heavy and rapid. The nest was fouled with her vomit. Once she stirred herself to get up, hunch her back, and rub her belly along the ground. Then she collapsed on the dead pups as if she wasn't even aware they were there.

"What'll we do?" Cristabel said. "She's so sick."

Philo blinked back tears. This was no time to cry. He had to think about what to do. "We'll have to take her to a vet."

"Where?"

"There's one on Panorama Avenue, a couple of blocks from our trailer court."

"How can we get her there?"

"I can carry her. She's not very big. But how can we pay for it?"

"There's still a lot of money in my piggy bank. I'll pay for it. We'd better hurry, though. She really looks bad."

They found an old burlap sack and wrapped Emerald in it, then hurried out of the yard and on toward Panorama Avenue. Philo thought they'd never get there. At times the dog was a dead weight in his arms. At other times she struggled to free herself. Although he was big for his age and strong, the fifteen minutes it took to get to the vet's seemed like an hour. Finally, there it was, a glass-fronted shop with the printing on the window, "Panorama Animal Hospital. F. A. March, Veterinarian." Philo and Cristabel hurried inside. Two women sat on plastic upholstered seats, obviously waiting for the vet. One held a case with a wailing cat in it. The other held only a leash.

As Philo and Cristabel glanced around for someone to help them, a glass window over a counter slid open. A skinny, sour-faced woman peered out. "You can pick up Cuddles now, Mrs. Peters," she said to the woman holding the leash. "Come right in." She motioned to a door beside the office window, then spoke into a loudspeaker. "Bring Cuddles Peters to the front, please." Then she turned to the woman with the cat. "Dr. March will be with you soon."

She was about to close the window when she noticed Philo and Cristabel. "Yes?"

Cristabel spoke up. "Our dog is awfully sick. In fact, it's really an emergency."

Philo said, "She just had puppies, but they all died. Now she's sick."

The woman gave a quick glance around the waiting room. "Isn't there anyone with you—a parent?"

Philo and Cristabel exchanged worried glances.

The woman said, "You'll have to get a parent. We can't take animals from minors, you know."

Philo hadn't known. It flashed through his head that he had certainly worn an appropriate hat today, his baseball cap. He felt as if the woman had just thrown him a fast ball and he'd struck out.

12

Too Many Emergencies

The sour-faced woman closed the glass window in the faces of Philo and Cristabel, obviously to deal with Cuddles Peters's owner inside the office and in private.

"What will we do?" Cristabel whispered.

Philo, completely at a loss, wished he had the answer. He stared down at the dog in his arms. Emerald hardly seemed conscious now. "We gotta find help right away." The vet had to be someplace beyond the office, Philo reasoned. If only he were braver, he'd walk right through the door.

As he so often did when he was afraid of something or someone, he thought of the many stories Poppy always told about his mother. In all of them she was like a knight facing dragons. She never backed away. She charged. She fought. He said to

Cristabel, "Come on," and made for the door near the window. Cristabel followed.

Because he needed both hands to hang on to Emerald, Philo asked Cristabel to open the door. When she did, he marched right through, acting much braver than he felt. He passed the desk where Cuddles Peters's owner was paying her bill and headed for the only open corridor he saw, Cristabel behind him.

The sour-faced woman glanced up as they passed. "Just a minute, Mrs. Peters," she said and took off after them. She was almost upon them when a tall, blond woman appeared in the hall. She wore what Philo thought of as a doctor's coat and carried a small, white poodle. When she spotted Philo and Cristabel, she said, "Well, what have we here?"

"It's an emergency," Philo said.

The woman from the desk tore forward and grabbed him by the shoulder. "These children don't have an adult with them, Dr. March. They pushed their way in here. I'll see that they don't bother you."

"An emergency, you say?" Dr. March stared at the dirty burlap-covered lump in Philo's arms and frowned. "Here, Mavis," she said, passing the poodle to her. "Take Mrs. Peters's dog to her."

"But, Dr. March—" Mavis said.

"You heard the boy—it's an emergency." To Philo and Cristabel, Dr. March said, "Take your dog into the first room to your left. I'll be right there."

As they made for the room, Philo could hear Mavis muttering her disapproval. Inside, he and Cristabel waited anxiously.

In a few moments Dr. March joined them and closed the door. "Put your dog up here," she said, patting a slick plastic-topped table.

Philo set Emerald gently down where the doctor indicated. Dr. March removed the burlap from around the dog, stirring up little clouds of dust. As she dropped the offensive wrapping in a wastebasket, she made a face and said, "Phew. Couldn't you find something cleaner than that?"

Philo and Cristabel traded guilt-stricken glances. Philo said again, "It was an emergency."

Emerald tried to stand, but her legs gave way beneath her. She was too weak to object as Dr. March took her temperature, examined her eyes and throat, and listened to her heartbeat. When the vet felt her abdomen, though, she winced. Dr. March said, "This is a very sick animal."

"She just had puppies," Philo offered.

"Yes, I can tell."

"They died," he added.

"Of course. She passed the disease to them."

"Will she get better?" Cristabel asked.

"I can't promise anything. If she has what I think she has, a cure is very difficult. She'll need shots and fluids, among other things."

"What's she got?" Philo asked.

"I'm almost certain she has canine hepatitis— which is really rare these days. You should have given your dog shots."

Again Philo and Cristabel exchanged guilty glances.

"But she was okay yesterday," Philo said.

"That's a characteristic of this disease. The animal may seem perfectly fine one day and be sick the next."

Cristabel said, "She couldn't get something like that from a dog that had it but was cured, could she?"

"If the dog had the disease recently, yes, she could definitely get it that way. Takes about a week or so to show up."

Philo had no time to ponder Cristabel's question, because the vet immediately called for an attendant to take Emerald away and start treatment. Then she turned to the two of them. "Where are your parents?"

Cristabel looked at Philo in a way that he knew meant she wanted him to answer. He said truthfully,

"My dad had to work. He's a school custodian. He had an emergency today."

Dr. March nodded thoughtfully. "I see—another emergency. Well, go give Mavis your names for her records. Phone me in an hour or so and I'll tell you how your dog—what's her name?"

"Emerald."

"I'll tell you how Emerald is doing."

They did as she said, giving Philo's address. Mavis seemed to take for granted that he and Cristabel were brother and sister. She took down the information, then said, "Well, if I were Dr. March I certainly wouldn't trust you. She's much too good-hearted." They left her mumbling to herself.

Outside, Philo said, "Why did you ask that question about a cured dog?"

Cristabel said, "Remember how I told you that Mopey was in the vet's for a while? The Whipples told my mother the name of what he had, and I couldn't remember it. Well, that's what he had. The minute Dr. March said the name, it came back to me."

If Mopey had had the disease, then, according to the vet, he had given it to Emerald. And if Mopey had given it to Emerald, it was all Philo's fault. If he'd left Mopey in his own yard, none of this would have happened.

"I guess it's our fault," Cristabel said.

"It's *my* fault," Philo said.

"Well, if I hadn't suggested keeping Mopey until the Whipples fixed their fence, he would never have met Emerald."

"But I was the one that left the gate open. And I didn't have to let Mopey follow me in the first place. No, it's my fault—all my fault."

With a tiny shrug, she said, "Well, if you insist."

Philo felt he owed it to Emerald to shoulder the blame himself. All the same, Cristabel might have argued just a little bit longer.

She had to return home to go shopping with her mother, so Philo volunteered to phone Dr. March to find out about Emerald.

"I'll call you just as soon as we get back from shopping," Cristabel said. "If you're not home, I'll know you're at Pepper Tree Acres, and I'll meet you there." She added optimistically, "I'll bet Emerald will be all right once she gets some medicine."

"I hope so," Philo said. He was glad to be alone for a while. He hated for anyone to see him cry.

Philo returned to the trailer and watched television to make his hour of waiting go faster. It didn't. He had left Panorama Animal Hospital around eleven o'clock. At the dot of twelve he phoned. Mavis, he felt, probably would have hung up on him except that he immediately said, "Dr. March said I should call her."

After several minutes Dr. March came on the line. When she did, she was not encouraging. "I don't want to get your hopes up. This is a very sick animal. I'll do everything I can, but it doesn't look good right now. Hold on—Mavis wants to talk to you."

Mavis's voice blasted in his ear. "I want to speak to one of your parents."

"There's only my dad."

"Then put him on."

"I can't. He's not here. He's at work."

"Then you have him call me the minute he gets home. This is most irregular—most irregular. We can't be having children bringing in pets whenever the notion strikes them. There has got to be an adult with them."

Philo promised to have his dad call, but he didn't really mean it. How could he tell Poppy what he'd been up to behind his back? Oh, it should all have been so easy, finding homes for a few dogs. Why did this have to happen and complicate everything? And it was his fault, all his fault.

Philo yanked off his baseball cap. He thought he'd never want to see it again. Look at all the bad that had happened today while he was wearing it.

He went through a drawer of the small cabinet that held his clothes and fished out his watch cap, his lucky cap. He put it on, feeling that now things would change for the better.

He was almost out the door, meaning to head for the corridor and his dogs, when the phone rang. Hoping it was the doctor again, only this time with good news, he dashed back to answer it. "Potts residence. Philo speaking," he said, the way Miss Jolly had taught him.

"Oh, Philo, honey, can I speak to your daddy?"

Marilyn. He'd have known that accent anyplace. What did *she* want? "He's not here," Philo said smugly. "He had an emergency at school. He'll be gone all day. Maybe all night, too." He hoped that would discourage her.

"Oh, I was plumb hopin' to catch him. I guess I'll just have to leave a message with you."

"Okay," Philo said.

"You just tell your daddy to be sure and call me tomorrow mornin'. I'll tell him then what time to pick me up."

Philo scowled. "You going someplace tomorrow?"

"My stars! Didn't he tell you? We're goin' to see *A Chorus Line.*"

"What's that?"

133

"Why, it's a show, honey—a musical."

"He didn't tell me we were gonna see a show."

There was a long silence. Finally she said, "It's kind of a grown-ups' show, honey. Your daddy and I thought we'd take in the matinee, then come on home and pick you up, and we'd all go someplace to dinner."

"Oh," he said. He didn't know what else to say. She was spoiling another Sunday for him and he hated her for it, wished she'd go back to Texas.

"You be sure and tell your daddy, hear?"

Philo said he would and hung up. What really hurt was that Poppy hadn't said one word about to-morrow. Of course, the emergency at school had probably driven everything else from his mind. All the same, he knew how Philo felt about their Sundays. But did that bother him? No. All he cared about was Marilyn Hotchkiss, didn't care about Philo at all.

Philo ripped the watch cap—the cap that had once belonged to his dad—from his head, wadded it into a ball like an old sock, and threw it at the couch. It landed on the floor. Well, let it stay there. Philo was too sad and mad and hurt to care. Besides, every hat he picked today was wrong. He just wouldn't wear one. Hats belonged to happy times anyhow. They should remind you of good things and fun days. Philo went out, hatless, and headed for Pepper Tree Street.

When he arrived at the house, only three of the dogs met him at the gate. Rajah was not among them. Worried, Philo tore through the front yard and around to the back patio, calling the dog's name. After a moment, he spotted Rajah, almost hidden, in an area near the block wall where weeds grew tall and dense. To his horror, Philo saw the dog retch, then vomit.

Not Rajah, too!

But how could that be? He'd been fine only a couple of hours ago. Or had he and Cristabel been so absorbed with Emerald that they hadn't noticed? Now Philo scrutinized the other dogs. They looked as frisky as ever.

Philo stood, helplessly staring at Rajah. Tears welled up in his eyes and spilled over to trickle down his cheeks. How could all this be happening to him? Why? All he'd wanted was to help the dogs, to do something really good for them. Instead, he'd hurt them—the five puppies, Emerald, and now Rajah.

He wiped the tears on the sleeve of his jacket. There was no time for them. He had to do something, had to get Rajah to Dr. March, and fast. But the dog was too big to carry. Philo had had enough trouble with Emerald. And why did Cristabel have to go shopping when he needed her? But she couldn't have helped him anyhow. What he had to have was the use of a car, and one bigger than Poppy's little Volkswagon.

As he tried to decide what to do, Philo led Rajah away from his mess. He hugged the animal to him and felt gratified to feel a weak response. Perhaps the dog wasn't too bad yet. Philo thought he wouldn't be able to bear it if anything happened to his favorite, Rajah, Royal Ruler of Pepper Tree Acres.

As hard as he searched his mind, he could think of only one person he could ask for help. He hated to do it, but he was desperate. "I'll be right back," he assured the dog. "I'll hurry." Then he was off, running all the way.

When he arrived, breathless, at his trailer court, he made for the pink mobile home in the space next to his trailer and hammered on the door. "Miss Jolly, you just gotta help me," he called. "I gotta get Rajah to the vet. He's awful sick. I need a car and Poppy's is too small. If you don't help him, he'll die."

In a moment, the door opened and Miss Jolly, wearing a stunned expression and an afro wig, peered out at him.

13

Miss Jolly Takes Charge

Miss Jolly drove a Checker, a great old ark of a car that looked like a taxi, and which, at some point, she'd had painted pink to match her mobile home. She seldom used the car for anything but her infrequent shopping trips. Philo thought her a terrible driver. She drove at one speed only, thirty-five miles an hour, which was always too slow or too fast for the traffic. He wondered why she never had an accident. Miss Jolly claimed a psychic had told her she had a good little spirit who sat on her right shoulder and looked after her.

She owned a pink pants suit that she usually wore whenever she used her car. Today she had just come back from her daily two-mile run, so she had on bright green jogging clothes and her athletic shoes. There was no time to change. She merely took a moment to grab her grape-purple velveteen trench coat, and she was ready. Philo was never sure whether people's heads turned to stare at the odd car or its driver.

He directed her to the house on Pepper Tree Street, wishing she would drive a little faster. As she turned off the main boulevard of the corridor, she said, "Your dad would be very worried about you, Philo, if he knew what you've been up to, coming to this dangerous spot every day, keeping an animal at a vacant house. You're just lucky I'm an animal lover. I don't know who else would come running out like this. And who's going to pay for the vet, I'd like to know? Your dad can't afford to pay for stray animals."

Philo listened in silence. He wasn't up to telling her the whole story. He would just have to let it unfold of itself, a little at a time. And it did. After she parked and went with him to the gate, three barking dogs filled in another part of the tale.

"I thought you said, 'dog,' " Miss Jolly said.

"Well, there's these three, too. I forgot to tell you."

Before she could comment, Cristabel, back from her shopping trip, came from behind the house and started toward them, then stopped abruptly as

138

her eyes settled on Miss Jolly. "Who's she?" Cristabel asked.

At the same time, Miss Jolly said, "Who's she?"

Still another part of the story came out as Philo introduced the two. "Rajah's sick," he told Cristabel. "Miss Jolly's gonna drive him to the vet."

"I was just going to tell you about Rajah. He's in the service porch, and he doesn't want to come out," she said.

"Then we better get him," Philo said. "You wait here, Miss Jolly. We'll be right back."

As Miss Jolly got acquainted with the other dogs, Philo and Cristabel hurried back to Rajah. Cristabel said, "If she's your friend I suppose I shouldn't say anything, but she certainly looks weird. I'll bet she'll call the SPCA, and they'll come and take the dogs to the pound."

"Oh, I don't think so. Miss Jolly's an animal lover. No animal lover would do a thing like that." He was more worried that Miss Jolly would tell his dad. Poppy would never let him come back here. Then what would happen to the dogs?

He put his worries aside to get their one leash and snap it on Rajah's collar. Then he and Cristabel, tugging, pushing, coaxing, finally got the dog outside. With their help, Rajah, unsteady on his feet, made it to the pink car.

"Oh, dear," Miss Jolly said as she watched them direct him into the back seat. "Poor doggie."

Rajah sank onto the plastic mat she'd had the foresight to stretch over the floor. Philo sat in back with him while Cristabel climbed in front with Miss Jolly.

Philo was afraid Rajah might panic when the car started, but either he had ridden in cars before or he was too sick to care. He neither budged when Miss Jolly revved the engine nor when she got it up to her customary thirty-five miles per. All the way to the animal hospital she kept saying, "I just don't know what to make of all this."

By the time they arrived at the vet's she had obviously come to terms with her confusion, because she was more than a match for Mavis. When the window slid open, Mavis's eyes moved from Philo to Cristabel to the sick Rajah, then from the top of Miss Jolly's afro, down over the purple velveteen trench coat, past the bright green jogging pants, and all the way to the soles of the athletic shoes.

"We gotta see Dr. March right away," Philo said. "It's an emergency."

Mavis paid him no attention. Instead, she said to Miss Jolly, "Are you with them?"

"Of course not," Miss Jolly said. When Mavis

turned to Philo and Cristabel with a scowl that plainly said she was not about to tolerate their presence without an adult a second time, Miss Jolly added, "Of course I am not with them. *They* are with me."

Mavis's mouth hung open as she turned back to Miss Jolly. She stared at the old woman for a moment, then closed her mouth and said, "I see. Well, please take a seat. It will be a few moments before Dr. March can see you."

She was about to slide the window closed when Miss Jolly moved nearer, scrutinized Mavis's face, then said, "My dear, you really should pay more attention to your skin. You could have a rather nice complexion if you did something about those large pores."

Mavis's hand automatically rose to her face. She peered at Miss Jolly as if examining *her* skin, which was perfect. Miss Jolly always said she was her own best advertisement.

"I'm an authority on skin, you know. You may have heard of me—Gretchen Jolly?"

Mavis, looking bewildered, moved her head from side to side.

"Well, I'm retired now, of course. But there isn't much I don't know about skin. In fact, I'm writing a book about it. I always say, 'God gave us only one skin, and we should all take care of it.' Next time I'm in, I'll bring you a little jar of a cream I devised with a cucumber base. It will do wonders for those pores. Of course, your liver spots are something else." The phone rang, so Mavis never did find out how to deal with her liver spots.

"She's weird," Cristabel whispered, nodding toward Miss Jolly.

"Yeah, I know," Philo said. "I guess I'm just used to her."

They were the only people in the waiting room now, so there were no other animals to disturb Rajah. Even so, the wait seemed like hours and hours to Philo. When Dr. March finally examined the dog, Philo's fears were confirmed. "It looks like another case of canine hepatitis," she said and immediately called an attendant who took Rajah off to start treatment. Philo, Cristabel, and Miss Jolly stared after him.

Dr. March said, "That dog doesn't seem to be in quite as bad shape as the first one, but nevertheless I don't want to give you false hopes. The disease is always serious."

"What first dog would you be talking about?" Miss Jolly asked.

Philo said quickly, "Emerald."

"Oh, Emerald," Miss Jolly said, but her eyes

were saying, *Philo Potts, what else have you been keeping from me?*

"How many dogs do you have, anyhow?" Dr. March asked.

"Five," Philo said.

"Really? Quite a few for one family. Well, maybe you'd better bring in the other three and let me check them. The disease is highly contagious."

So Miss Jolly, Philo, and Cristabel drove back to the house on Pepper Tree Street, picked up the remaining dogs, who objected loudly all the way, and took them to the animal hospital.

After Dr. March examined and tested them, she said, "The two males show definite symptoms. I'd like to keep them until I'm sure. I can't see anything wrong with the female, though. You may take her home, but do keep an eye on her." She turned Princess Starlight over to them.

Philo snapped the leash onto her collar, and they all started to walk past the desk and out. Mavis shot to her feet. "Just a minute there," she cried, waving a paper at them. "That will be eighteen dollars before you can take the dog. That includes the office call, of course."

Philo and Cristabel looked first at each other, then at Miss Jolly. Miss Jolly said, "Philo, do you have eighteen dollars?"

143

Philo shook his head.

She said to Cristabel, "Do you?"

"I think so, but it's in my piggy bank."

Miss Jolly sighed. "Well, I guess I'm 'it' then. How much are the other dogs going to cost?"

Mavis said, "I can't tell yet."

"Well, make a rough guess," Miss Jolly said.

Mavis shrugged. "From other like cases, I would imagine the care for each animal could run in the neighborhood of two or three hundred dollars."

Philo and Cristabel exchanged horrified glances.

Miss Jolly said, "That's what I suspected." She drew a checkbook from a big pouchy handbag, wrote a check, tore it off, and handed it to Mavis. "You may as well take my phone number. I'll be anxious to hear how the dogs are doing." After she gave Mavis her number, she said, "I'll be sure and bring a jar of my cucumber cream next time I'm in the neighborhood. It performs absolute miracles. What's more, I can sell it at bargain prices because, of course, there are no middlemen."

Mavis's eyes narrowed to suspicious slits. "How much is it?"

"Only fifteen dollars. And I also have a superb elixir that will get rid of those liver spots on your hand and that one on your forehead. I'll bring some of that as well."

"And how much is that?" Mavis asked.

"Practically a gift—three dollars."

As they left, Philo glanced back to see Mavis examining her face in a small hand mirror. He said, "Fifteen dollars and three more makes eighteen. That's the same amount as the bill."

"Yes, it is, isn't it?" Miss Jolly said in a tone that suggested the world was full of the loveliest of coincidences. Outside, as she stared down at the dog, her tone changed. "What did you say her name is?"

"Princess Starlight," Cristabel said.

Miss Jolly shook her head. "And what are we going to do with her?"

"We'll have to take her back to the yard," Philo said.

"We'll do no such thing," Miss Jolly said. "Neither of you children is to go anyplace near that part of town again." She turned to Cristabel. "Can't *you* take the dog?"

"My mother won't let me. She doesn't like dogs. In fact, she hates them."

Miss Jolly said to Philo, "And you can't have an animal in that trailer of yours. It's against the rules of the court."

"*I* can't have one, but *you* can. The rules say it's

okay in mobile homes as long as the dog isn't big. Princess Starlight is real little."

"Philo, you know I don't want a dog, and you know why I don't want a dog. Besides, this animal is a stray who's been living wild. I'm sure she isn't even housebroken. And there's no yard as such, so she'd have to be taken out for walks several times a day. And there are a hundred or so other reasons why I should not take her."

"Well, maybe you could take her just until we find her a home," Philo said.

"I said there were plenty of reasons why I should *not* take her, but it looks as though I'm 'it' again. However, you two had better start looking hard for a home for that royal animal, because I refuse to keep her for more than a couple of days."

They promised, and as they all piled into the pink Checker, Miss Jolly reminded them of the debt they were running up with Dr. March. "With four dogs, the cost could easily go up to a thousand dollars even if the dogs don't get better. Just where do you think you're going to get that kind of money?"

"Oh, I know I don't have anything like that in my piggy bank," Cristabel said.

"What'll they do to us if we can't pay?" Philo asked.

"Probably sue your parents," Miss Jolly said.

Cristabel moaned. "Oh, my mother will be so mad at me."

Philo couldn't imagine how Poppy would react. He was easy-going about most things but careful with money. He had to be, because they didn't have that much. No, there was no way they could come up with a fortune like that. But how could you worry about something like money when you had all those sick animals to worry about? You could only do so much worrying at one time. He said, "Please don't say anything to Poppy, Miss Jolly."

She took her eyes from the road to glance at him quickly, a worried expression on her face. "I can't promise that. Your dad *has* to know. I want you to tell him, Philo. If *you* don't, I *will*."

Philo nodded, but he didn't say anything.

Cristabel said, "Oh, I hope the dogs don't die. If they'd just get better, it would be worth anything we had to go through."

Philo thought she looked as miserable as he felt. "I tried so hard to help them," he said, verging on tears. "Instead, all I did was make things worse. Now they're sick and they'll most likely die and I'll owe all that money and they'll sue Poppy, and everything is just awful."

"Now, now," Miss Jolly said. "What's done is done. Besides, you did what you did because you

147

cared about those dogs. You thought you were doing what was best for them. We all make some of our biggest mistakes trying to do what we think is best for those we love."

She drove along, silent for a time, then said, "I remember a situation very similar to this one on 'Private Worlds.' " She appeared to be mulling over that situation for a time. "Yes, that just might be an idea."

Miss Jolly and her soap operas! She always thought everything was just a story on television. Well, it wasn't. There were real things that happened that didn't work out like stories.

Miss Jolly, sounding as if she had already forgotten the problem at hand, said, "I should have said something to that Dr. March about the frown lines in her forehead. I have a wonderful relaxing mask that could do her a world of good."

14 ⤲

Pictures Don't Lie;
Only People Lie

It was Sunday and the worst day of his life, Philo was sure.

"Did you tell your dad?" Miss Jolly had asked the moment he'd shown up in her mobile home.

"Not yet. I'll tell him tonight."

"Philo Potts! Remember what I said. If you don't tell him, I will."

"I'll tell him, I'll tell him," he said crossly. Why did she have to keep at him when he was feeling so miserable?

On last report, Emerald was no better, Rajah was worse, one of the other males definitely had the disease, the second was still under observation. And the bill was climbing. Only Star, as Miss Jolly chose to call the dog, was well and happy.

"She's the smartest little thing," Miss Jolly said.

149

"I caught her once last night about to do her business in the house. I took her outside and told her never to try that again. I said, 'You just tell me when you have to go out.' Do you know, the next time she *did*—stood at the door and whined. I believe she understands me."

Philo was glad someone was happy, because he wasn't. He was reminded today of that other Sunday when Marilyn had asked his dad to drive her to the valley. That was the day Mopey had followed him to the corridor, the day this had all begun. If Marilyn had only stayed out of their lives, none of this would have happened.

"It's all her fault," Philo said as he helped Miss Jolly work on the blue sky of her jigsaw puzzle. Anything to kill time.

"What's whose fault?" Miss Jolly asked.

"Marilyn Hotchkiss. I woulda never got mixed up with the dogs, and they wouldn't be sick if she didn't take Poppy away that Sunday."

"Now don't you go blaming your dad's girlfriend for something *you* did."

Philo scowled. "What do you mean—girlfriend?"

"Philo Potts, you needn't get your hackles up. It's perfectly natural to call a woman a man takes out on dates his girlfriend."

"Those aren't dates. She asks him point-blank all the time to go places, and Poppy can never say no when someone asks him anything point-blank. That's how he is. I bet she asked him point-blank to go to that show today."

"Your dad isn't that simpleminded. If he went, it was because he wanted to go. And high time, too. He's still a young man."

"He's not young—he's thirty-four!"

Miss Jolly rolled her eyes. "And over the hill, of course." Then she fixed him with her most piercing gaze. "You listen to me, Philo. Your mother has been gone for years. Even if he never says so, your dad can't help but be a little lonely. He's had to be both mother and father to you. Until now, he's never even gone off on his own with people his own age."

"Why does he *have* to?"

"People just do, that's all. If your dad has met someone he likes to be with, you should be glad for him."

"Well, all I got to say is he better not try marrying her."

"Philo, Philo—" Miss Jolly said, shaking her head. "It's natural for a man your father's age to enjoy the company of a woman. And it's natural for him to want to marry again. You're just going to have to try to understand that. If you gave yourself a chance you might even find that this Marilyn isn't half bad."

"Well, she may not be half bad, but she sure isn't half good either."

"Now don't tell me again that she isn't as pretty as your mother."

"Well, she isn't!"

"I told you, Philo, photographs often lie."

"I don't see why you keep saying that. You never did know my mother."

"That's true, I didn't. But many's the time I saw her coming and going. She was living here, you know, before she went away, right up to that last day."

Miss Jolly was as bad as Cristabel. With Cristabel, people didn't die, they passed away. With Miss Jolly, they went away.

Miss Jolly's eyes glazed over as she stared off into another time. "Why, I saw her that very morning, going off in a taxi. And if I hadn't heard you and called the police, you'd have lain there all day, crying your baby's heart out until your dad came home."

"Was that the day she died?"

"That was—" Miss Jolly's eyes cleared and she stared at him as if she had forgotten he was there. "Why, yes—yes, of course."

152

Philo had a sad vision of his mother in great pain, stepping out of the cab and into the hospital where doctors and nurses rushed her into the operating room, somewhat like one of Miss Jolly's soap operas. The vision stopped short of anyone's cutting into her. He didn't care to think about that. She had died suddenly, Poppy said, of a ruptured appendix. "I wonder why she took a taxi instead of an ambulance. Didn't she even call Poppy?"

Miss Jolly, her eyes on the jigsaw pieces, said, "I really don't know."

Philo thought about it. "I guess she probably couldn't get him."

"That's very likely the case."

"If you saw her so many times, how come you don't know if she looked like her picture?"

"I never said I didn't know."

"I guess you don't think she did, else you wouldn't always be saying that pictures lie."

Miss Jolly gave a deep sigh. "Yes, I *did* say that. But I've changed my mind. It really isn't pictures that lie. Oh, they may exaggerate a bit, but they don't lie. Only people lie."

"What's that supposed to mean?"

"It means I am not going to say another word. Anything you want to know about your mother you'll have to ask your dad. And you'd better tell him about the dogs. If you don't, it's just the same as lying." She got up from the card table and went over to her antique desk. "Now, I have a very important letter to write, so please be quiet so I can think."

Miss Jolly spent what was left of the afternoon composing her letter. Philo worked absently on the jigsaw puzzle, trying unsuccessfully to focus his thoughts on something other than Miss Jolly's words.

Before she went away. I saw her that very morning, going off in a taxi. Pictures don't lie. Only people lie. You'd have lain there all day, crying your baby's heart out. She was living here right up to that last day. She went away. People lie. She went away.

Philo kept mulling over the sentences, shifting the sequence around, hoping he could make the meaning come out differently. Until his dad came home, he spent the time pretending deep concentration on the puzzle, all his fearful thoughts and wild guesses locked tightly inside him, festering away.

When he and Poppy were alone in their trailer, Philo could hardly contain himself as Poppy said, "You all ready? I dropped Marilyn off at her house. We're going to her place instead of a restaurant. She wants to fix dinner for us."

Philo said, "You go. I don't want to."

His dad looked anxiously into his face. "You mad or something?"

Philo shook his head.

"Then what's the matter?"

"Nothing."

"Aw, come on, I know you better than that. What have I done now?"

Philo blurted, "You never told me my mother went away in a taxi, that's what!"

Poppy's eyes narrowed. "Who told you that—Miss Jolly?"

Philo nodded.

Poppy, standing near the pass-through between living area and kitchen, brought a curled fist down hard on the counter. "She shouldn't have done that. She had no right. She knew why I—" He broke off. "What else did she say?"

Philo didn't answer. He had desperately hoped Poppy would say, "Well, of course she went off in a taxi. After all I've told you about Honeybunch. You know how she was—independent, brave, even on the last day of her life." From Poppy's manner, Philo could tell that what he suspected was true. In a quavery voice, he said, "You lied to me."

Looking weary now, Poppy walked over to the sofa and sank down upon it. He stared at Philo in silence, as if at a loss for words.

Philo stood glaring down at him, fists doubled, tears threatening. "You lied to me! You told me she was dead! And it was a lie! She's not dead at all. And that's about the biggest kind of lie anybody could tell. A person could get struck down dead for telling a lie like that. I bet you just don't want me to see her because I might like her better than you." Philo was striking out wildly with all the verbal punches he could think of, his voice rising shrilly. "And all those stories—I bet those were lies, too."

He glanced over to the picture on the television set, at the words that said, "Best Wishes, Joan." *Pictures sometimes lie.* No! *Only people lie.* "And that isn't even her picture, is it? You lied about that, too." Now tears streaked down his cheeks.

"Philo, listen to me," his dad said. "Will you just keep quiet a minute and listen to my side of it?"

Philo fell silent and wiped the tears from his cheeks with the back of a hand. He stared at his dad belligerently.

"Okay, I admit it, I lied. But, in a way, I didn't. I mean, even if your mom is alive—and I don't know that she is—she's dead to the two of us. She took off in a cab, all right, and I never saw her again. She might as well be dead."

Philo's dead mother had always seemed very much alive to him. Now that it appeared she was still living, he felt as if she had just died. "How come Aunt Gert never told me she was alive?"

"I wouldn't let her. I guess I was bitter about a lot of things after Joan left. Gert never did like her anyhow, so she thought you were just as well off not knowing."

Once she was Honeybunch; now she was Joan. "I bet you were mean to her."

Poppy sighed. "No. It wasn't like that at all. It was just that she was so young—eighteen when you were born. It was hard on her, living in this trailer. I didn't have my job at school then. I was working for a supermarket, stocking shelves. Wasn't making a heck of a lot. She wanted better. Now I can't blame her. She was a good-looking kid. Deserved better."

Philo glanced at the picture again. His dad's eyes followed his. "You're right," Poppy said. "That's a picture of an actress who was on some old soap opera Miss Jolly used to watch. Miss Jolly wrote her one of her famous letters and got the photo back. She didn't want it, so when I noticed it was signed 'Joan,' same name as your mother, I asked her for it.

"I didn't have one picture of your mom, because she took our snapshot album with her. I figured, if nothing else, a kid needed a picture of his mom. Miss Jolly didn't think much of the idea, but I believed I knew best what was right for you.

157

"And all those stories—well, maybe I did exaggerate some. But it's true I hurt my leg that time and she had to go get help. And it's true she was pretty brave about a lot of things—more than me. Like, she loved to ride roller coasters, and they scare me to death. A hero, I'm not. I figure kids need heroes as much as they need mothers. So, okay, I decided my boy was gonna have both."

He got up, took the picture from the top of the television set, and carried it into the kitchen area where he dropped it in a wastebasket. "I guess we don't need that anymore."

Philo watched with mixed emotions. He wanted never to see that smiling face again, and yet the empty spot on top of the television set gave him an even deeper sense of loss.

His dad said, "Thought I was doing something good for you. I guess Miss Jolly was right—it was a mistake. I'm sorry, Slugger. I didn't mean to do you harm. You gotta believe that." He waited in silence, as if expecting a response from Philo. When none came, he said, "Can't go back and change it all now. We just gotta live with it. Come on, go wash your face, and we'll go over to Marilyn's. She'll be waiting for us."

Philo shook his head. "You go ahead. I don't feel like it."

"But you gotta eat."

"I'm not hungry."

"Then I'll stay home."

"No, that's okay. Go ahead."

"No, I'm staying home. We better talk some more. Just let me call Marilyn first and tell her we won't be over. Okay?"

Philo shrugged.

While his dad talked to Marilyn, he stared into space, trying not to think. A phrase here and there penetrated his consciousness. "Look, something important's come up . . . gotta talk to my boy . . . straighten things out."

When Poppy finally hung up, he said, "Marilyn says she understands. She's got a chicken casserole all ready to go into the oven. She wants me to run over and get it so's we'll have something to eat. Only take a few minutes. That okay with you?"

Philo nodded indifferently.

"Maybe by the time I come back you'll be able to forgive your old nerd of a dad."

Soon after Poppy left, the phone rang. It was Miss Jolly. "Philo, dear," she said, "I've just heard from Dr. March, and I'm afraid the news isn't good."

"They're all dead," he said in a flat voice.

"No, dear, not all of them—only the one you called Emerald. Dr. March tried very hard to save her, but it just wasn't possible. She was a bit older than the other dogs."

"They'll die, too. I know they will. And it's all my fault."

"Now don't go blaming yourself, dear. You did what you did out of love, and no one can fault that. Even if you did make a mistake in the way you went about it, no one had a better reason."

She went on talking, but Philo didn't listen. He hung up the phone, put on his jacket, left the trailer, and took off into a misting night. As he walked up the street, his hand rose unthinkingly to smooth the brim of his hat. He wasn't wearing one. Well, he was right to go bareheaded. Hats were for happy times. This was not a happy time. Emerald was dead. The other dogs were dying. A little while ago, he'd had a wonderful mother. Now she was dead, too. Poppy had just killed her.

15

A Terrifying Experience

Philo settled himself on the floor of the kitchen, atop some old burlap sacks that smelled strongly of mildew. He couldn't bring himself to go deeper into the house on Pepper Tree Street. Without the presence of the dogs, the place seemed lonely, even unfriendly. Yet he could think of nowhere else to spend the night, and outside a heavy mist was falling. In the darkness, listening to the strange creaks and unidentifiable noises that made the vacant house seem alive, Philo felt chilled and uneasy.

This was not the ideal spot for thinking, but think he must. He had the feeling that if he could just sort out things he would find the answer to why God saw fit to send all this suffering his way. He thought about the dogs and he thought about

Poppy. Something kept nudging a corner of his brain, trying to link the two. No, he couldn't do it. His head was such a jumble that there was no way he could wrap his mind around those painful subjects right now.

Besides, he had to plan his future. Tomorrow he would head for parts unknown. Alaska maybe. Maybe Mexico. No, not Mexico. There weren't enough jobs there, he'd heard, and he'd have to have a job. What could he do? Well, lots of things. He was big and he was strong. He'd say he was fourteen. That ought to be old enough to get work. But what did people do in Alaska? He had no idea. And how would he get there? The only way. Hitch rides. Poppy said he must never hitch rides. But he no longer had to do what Poppy said. From now on, he was on his own.

Maybe he'd make his way to the docks and stow away on one of the big freighters that went clear around the world. Yes, he'd like that. He could send Cristabel cards from all the ports they stopped at. Of course, he wouldn't sign his name—couldn't take a chance on anyone's finding out where he was. He would just put down "A Friend." That would drive her crazy.

Yes, the freighter sounded good. It would hit a lot of hot countries, he was sure. Right now, in this unheated house, listening to the steady patter of rain that had set up, that sounded good, too.

Although his brain rejected the idea of food, his stomach growled noisily. There were still a few dollars in his pocket, left over from the dog-food money. Tomorrow he'd have a fine breakfast at McDonald's or someplace like that, then head for the docks. With his future settled, he tried to sleep to make the night turn quickly into morning. Instead, the sting of fresh wounds kept his mind painfully active and awake.

All a lie.

He could not wrench his thoughts from that fact. It was as if a part of him had disappeared and he was not who he'd thought he was but someone else. He had always been an ordinary kid, sure, but there was that other little piece he'd owned. It was magic, it was beautiful, and it was gone.

Why had she left him all alone like that—a little baby, crying in a trailer? What kind of a person would do such a thing? It wasn't so much that she maybe didn't like him or maybe couldn't stand babies, but just to go off in a taxi and leave a poor little kid all alone in a trailer, crying its baby's heart out— that was what was so sad. That poor baby. How could she do it?

Feeling forsaken, Philo began to cry, softly at first. Once started, the tears refused to stop. He cried until deep sobs shook his body. He cried and cried, unashamedly because no one could see him, cried until he was exhausted, until, at some point, he drifted into sleep.

He awoke with a start, wondering why his bed felt so hard, smelled so bad. Then it all came back to him. He was not in his bed but on the kitchen floor of the house on Pepper Tree Street. And it was dark there. And cold. And lonely. He pushed the button that made his Timex light up. Eleven-thirty. He wished now that he could turn time back a day. He would be at home in the trailer, warm, cozy, and asleep in the top bunk. Emerald would still be alive, and he would know nothing about the lies Poppy had told.

His mind went over their conversation again. It struck him now that someplace on this earth a woman lived who was his mother. He couldn't possibly like her, though, not a woman who would leave a husband like Poppy and a tiny baby.

"Tell me about the time you and Honeybunch did this or that." How often he had begged his dad for those stories. It was like a game. He realized now that he had always felt that way about them. They were fun. They were even play. But were they real? No. People just didn't talk about real-life things that happened to them in quite that way. He wondered if some part of him had always known.

In spite of all his hurt, Philo knew his dad loved him. That was the kind of thing you always knew, couldn't help knowing. But Poppy shouldn't have lied, Philo thought. It was wrong, dead wrong.

Miss Jolly's words came back to him. *You'd better tell your dad about the dogs. If you don't, it's just the same as lying.* If she was right, then he had lied, too. Deep inside him, Philo knew his dad had meant him well, even as he had meant only well for the dogs. Then why had it all turned out so badly?

Before he could pursue this line of thought, he was aware of strange noises. He sat up, alert now, listening hard. From someplace nearby came the sound of running feet. More than one person, Philo was sure, and they had to be on the path that led around to the back of the house. Philo quickly got up. He had used his key to get into the house but had given no thought to locking up from the kitchen side. As he groped awkwardly in his pocket, the door to the service porch rattled noisily, sounding as if someone was trying to get in. At the same time,

165

Philo heard the swish of tires over wet pavement. What was going on? Cars never used Pepper Tree Street because of its dead end.

Philo finally drew the key from his pocket and, with shaking hands, turned it in the lock. A moment later he could make out the sound of the door to the service porch opening and closing.

"Hey, how about that, Jess," a male voice said. "We didn't even have to break in. That door just opened real neat, like it was waitin' for us."

"Keep your voice down, you turkey. You want those pigs out there to hear you?"

The voice lowered. "Aw, don't call me that, Jess. How was I supposed to know there'd be a cop in that bar? The guy didn't even have on a uniform or nothin'."

"Shuddup."

His heart thudding, Philo listened through the door, but the two fell silent. He heard a car pull into the drive, then back out. In a few moments the sound of the engine faded away in the distance.

"You hear that, Jess? They're gone. Let's get outa here."

"Man, when they handed out brains, they sure missed you, Louie. What do you think those pigs are gonna do? Go home and go to bed now? Well, they

166

ain't. They'll be cruisin' all around these parts for hours. We stay right here till it's safe."

Philo felt more frightened than ever. He was hoping they would leave, and fast. Those two must have done something bad to have the cops after them.

"I sure think we oughta go, Jess."

"No way. I listened to you enough tonight, Louie." As if imitating Louie, he said in a singsong rhythm, snapping fingers to the beat, " 'I'm gonna jack me a car, then jack me a bar. I'm gonna jack me a car, then jack me a bar.' You're a weed-head, Louie. You don't think straight. I told you it was a lousy night for it."

"How was I supposed to know it was gonna rain?"

"It ain't the rain, you turkey. Aagh, never mind. Let's just get inside the house. I gotta stretch out. I'm so bushed I couldn't run another foot."

Philo's stomach tightened. They were coming in! But how could they? The door was locked. The key! He had left it in the lock. They would do exactly as he had done days earlier. Slip something under the door, push the key out to fall on it, then pull the something through with the key. He tried, oh, so quietly, to remove the key, but his hands shook. To his ears the clinky noise he made sounded like the sham battle at the end of Fourth of July fireworks. He had to give up.

On the other side of the door, Jess's voice, sounding startled, said, "What was that?"

"Mice maybe."

"Maybe. Maybe not. Come on, let's get this door open."

"Sure, Jess. This kinda lock is a cinch to pick. I could do it with my eyes closed."

Philo backed away from the door in terror. What would those guys do to him if they found him? Something bad, he was sure. Quietly, he made his way through the dark and farther into the house. He'd thought he knew where all the rooms were, but in the blackness everything seemed different. Finally, he reached the staircase. As he began tiptoeing up, the slam of a door told him they were already in the kitchen.

When Philo reached the upper story, he could hear steps echoing through the empty rooms below. He felt his way along the hall until he reached one of the bedrooms. Inside, floorboards creaked beneath his feet, but there was nothing he could do about it. His hands groped along the walls until he found a closet. He hid inside.

Only a few minutes passed before feet thudded

up the stairs. Philo guessed the intruders meant to search through every room. With both hands, he held onto the knob of the closet door, planning to put all his strength to work if anyone tried to open it.

He could hear the two moving about, covering the floor quickly, the sounds coming closer and closer, until finally they were in the room where he was hiding.

Louie's voice. "I told ya it was mice."

Jess now. "Yeah, you told me." He fell silent, then in a moment said, "What's in there?"

Philo's grip tightened on the doorknob. His heart was pounding so hard he was sure they could hear it. Then he felt someone try to turn the knob. He held on with all his strength.

"Locked," Louie said.

"Well, ain't that in-ter-es-ting," Jess said, giving equal emphasis to each syllable. "Now, how do ya suppose someone could lock a door that don't have no lock?"

"Hey, yeah, you're right, Jess."

Philo felt a powerful tug that wrenched the door open, caught him off balance, and threw him to the closet floor. In spite of the light from a small pocket flashlight shining in his eyes, he could see a gun pointed at his head.

"Well, well, well," Jess said. "Now, ain't that in-ter-es-ting."

"It's a kid," Louie said.

Philo shrank back, indeed feeling very much a kid. He would have given anything to be in the trailer, asleep in the top bunk, Poppy below, and dreaming instead of living this nightmare.

"Get up, kid," Jess said. "Louie, you bring him downstairs. I wanna be able to get out of this joint in a hurry if we have to."

As Philo got up, Louie grabbed the collar of his jacket and shoved him ahead. "Git!"

Philo saw nothing but the glint of a knife pointed at his throat.

Louie pushed him along. "Downstairs! Get a move on!"

Jess, holding the flashlight, was already at the bottom of the staircase. Philo started down, picking his way slowly in the dark. Suddenly the knife pricked his neck, and panic shot through him. He jumped away, slipped, and went hurtling down the stairs to land at the bottom, bruised and scared.

He heard Jess swear and say, "Can't you do nothin' right, you turkey?" In a second he was beside Philo, pulling him roughly to his feet. "Whatcha doin', kid—runnin' away? I bet you got a little bread on you to do somethin' like that. How about it?"

Breath knocked out of him, Philo opened his mouth but nothing came out. In the dim light, all he could make out were two men of about seventeen or eighteen years old, both with long stringy hair.

As Louie joined them, Jess said, "Search this geek."

"Sure," Louie said agreeably. "Hey, Jess, 'long as we gotta hole up here for a while, let's have us some fun with the kid. Know what I mean?"

Now Philo was terrified. He couldn't guess what Louie's idea of fun was, but he knew beyond a doubt that it would be the worst thing that had ever happened to him in his life. In seconds, Louie had stripped Philo of everything he valued materially, the Timex watch, the wallet that had been a present from Poppy, the three dollars inside it, as well as the priceless two-dollar bill.

"Man, that is some take," Jess said sarcastically.

"Yeah," Louie said, a hard edge to his voice now. "You shoulda had somethin' better on you, kid. We mighta been real nice to you then. A coupla bucks don't do my disposition no good. I get real mean. You know what I do to guys that only come up with a coupla bucks?"

Philo, his eyes wide with fear, moved his head from side to side.

With the back of his hand, Louie struck Philo

171

a blow that rocked him off his feet and sent him sprawling over the floor. His head reeled, his cheek stung from the impact of Louie's hand, and his body pained from the bruises of the fall downstairs. Tears gathered in his eyes but refused to fall, perhaps because he had cried so much earlier.

"That's just the beginning," Louie said.

Philo glanced up to see Louie striding toward him. At that moment, the small flashlight in Jess's hand flickered and went out. Louie swore.

Jess said, "Cool it, Louie. It's only the batteries. I got more in my pocket."

As he tinkered with the flashlight, a sudden draft of fresh air scuttled through the room. An eerie light lit the entrance to the kitchen. In the doorway loomed a creature that looked like a gigantic insect straight out of some horror movie. Light shone through transparent wings that billowed out as if the creature were about to take flight. Arched around its fuzzy head, a halo glowed. The monster brandished a weapon that glistened like some magical sword of old. The sight was stunning and horrifying. All the occupants of the room stood transfixed, staring at the thing as it peered into the darkness.

Philo heard Jess whisper to Louie, "We're invaded. Let's split."

There was no way they could get by the creature. Although they moved softly, Philo could almost feel them shrinking away from the kitchen door, then into the recesses of the house, where an occasional bumping noise gave away their presence.

"Philo Potts, is that you in there?" a familiar voice called.

Philo gasped. Now he recognized the monster. The eerie light had played strange tricks with Miss Jolly's transparent-plastic, hooded raincape and the umbrella that she had carefully striped with iridescent tape for visibility on a rainy night.

Philo scrambled to his feet, stumbled across the kitchen floor toward her. As he reached her side, he saw the figure just behind her. In another moment, Philo threw himself into a pair of strong, protective arms. "Poppy, oh, Poppy, I want to go home," he moaned.

At the same time, a voice blasted, "Come out with your hands raised. We've got the place surrounded."

16 ~

The Preclusion

The day was warm and summer-like, so Philo decided to eat his lunch outdoors on the school patio. His cousin Todd and two other boys were supposed to join him after they'd bought food in the cafeteria. Philo chose an empty table and turned chairs down to save them places.

As he sat down and pulled a bologna sandwich from his lunchbox, he spied Cristabel coming toward him, wearing her sweetest smile. That surprised him. She hadn't spoken to him for the better part of a week. He knew she was mad because her picture hadn't appeared in the paper beside his.

He could still see the headline, "Doggie Dogooder Leads to Capture of Thugs," and above that, the picture of himself, wearing his alpine hat, Miss

Jolly, wearing her silver-blond wig, and Princess Starlight, wearing a look of bewilderment and a new red-plaid doggie coat.

"Mind if I sit here?" Cristabel said now, pointing to an empty seat across from him.

What could he say? The chair wasn't turned down. He said, "It's a free country." After all, why should he be nice to her? Everyone had made a big fuss over him except her. All she had done was turn up her already turned-up nose.

He noticed that she kept staring at him strangely. Finally she said, "What's that thing on your head?"

He'd almost forgotten he'd put on his new hat before coming outside. "It's a hat. A car dealer was giving them away."

"That's a hat!" It was not a question.

"It's just for fun. I was lucky to get one. They only gave out a couple of hundred, and they were gone in twenty minutes. I like it because it makes people laugh."

Obviously it didn't make Cristabel laugh. She stared again at the beanie with pinwheel atop, turning smartly in the breeze, and sighed. Philo wasn't sure what the sigh meant. Cristabel sat down and placed a white paper bakery bag as well as her lunchbox on the table. She opened the box, took out a sandwich, and daintily unwrapped it. "It's baked chicken on my dad's homemade bread. Want half?"

Philo could see crisp green lettuce between the slices and creamy mayonnaise oozing out. It looked delicious. He said crossly, "I don't like chicken." After all, it was the principle of the thing.

Immediately she opened the white bag and held it out to him. "Maybe you'd like a napoleon for dessert. They're very good."

"How would you know?" he snapped. "You don't even eat them."

She patiently smiled her phony smile again. "You're right, I don't. But everyone else does, and they all say they're wonderful."

He was about to refuse her generosity a second time, but a sweet fragrance wafted out of the bag and up into his nostrils. He decided that once a day ought to be enough for anyone to stand on principle. "Well, I might just have one." He helped himself to the sticky pastry, placed it on his discarded sandwich bag, and licked off the bit of icing that stuck to his fingers. Delicious. His mood softened. "You know, it wasn't my fault your picture didn't get in the paper," he said a little defensively. "I did tell the reporter about you."

Now Cristabel's smile vanished and a scowl

took its place. "I noticed. I precluded that the eleven-year-old friend who was mentioned once, way down in the article, was me."

"What's that mean—precluded?"

"It means I supposed or guessed it was me—I mean, I. Of course, I could be wrong."

"It was you all right. I didn't give the reporter your name because I knew you didn't want your folks to know." As Cristabel mulled that over, Philo guessed she was consumed with jealousy because she hadn't shared his fame. On the other hand, by the serious look on her freckled face, he supposed—or was it precluded?—she was thinking about how her parents would have reacted if she'd been found out.

"How about your dad? What did he do to you?" she asked.

"Oh, he gave it to me good." That was only half true. His dad had obviously felt so guilty about causing Philo to run away and was so relieved to find him that the story of the dogs seemed less important than it might have otherwise. Oh, it was important all right, but in a different way.

"You shoulda told me," Poppy had said.

Philo said, "But if I *did* you wouldn't've let me go there. Or you would've called the pound."

"You're right that I wouldn't let you go near

that part of town. But you're wrong about the dogs. I understand how you feel about them. I would've tried to figure out something short of the pound. Stray animals are a problem for the whole city, Slugger. You should never try to cover up something like that. That's wrong."

Philo blurted, "I bet it's no more wrong than what you did. You were covering up, too—about her." He found it difficult now to say "Mother" or "Honeybunch."

The hurt look in his dad's eyes made Philo wish he could take back the words. Poppy said, "What it amounts to is that neither one of us trusts the other to have any good sense. That's what it amounts to."

Philo knew his dad was right. They had both deceived each other. But in spite of his hurt, in spite of his feeling of loss, Philo couldn't have stopped loving his dad even if he'd wanted to.

Now as he looked at Cristabel, he decided that, yes, his dad had let him off easily. But only because of the circumstances. And he had no intention of telling Cristabel about those now. Or ever. The truth was he had never meant to give her name to the reporter. He'd had no idea the article would make him famous. Instead, he'd thought he was cleansing his soul in confession for his wicked deeds. Actually,

178

it was a pretty heroic thing he'd done, taking the blame all by himself, but somehow he didn't think she'd see it that way, so he said, "I didn't give the reporter your name because I didn't want to see you get punished the way I did."

She looked at him sharply. "Why? What happened to you?"

"I'd rather not talk about it." Let her make what she wanted out of that.

She studied him as if looking for scars or flogging marks, or, at the very least, bruises. Finally she said, "I preclude you did the right thing, not giving my name. It's not that I'm worried about my father. He's a pussy cat. It's my mother. She'd kill me."

"That's what I figured," Philo said.

"In fact, I preclude we might as well be friends again."

Philo precluded the same. "Sure."

With that out of the way, Cristabel offered him another napoleon, which he took, then she set about satisfying her curiosity. "I don't understand how the newspaper people knew about the dogs. Did you tell them?"

Philo, nibbling on his pastry, shook his head. "Uh uh—Miss Jolly. Remember her?"

Cristabel rolled her eyes. "Who could forget her?"

"She wrote a letter to the editor, telling him about the dogs, and about how we tried to find homes for them, and about how they got sick, and all about the bill and how we didn't have the money to pay it. That's how he got interested."

"The paper said you were running away. Why were you doing that?"

"Aw, I wasn't running away. That's just reporter talk. It makes a better story that way."

"Then what were you doing in the house so late?"

"I was—well, I was—well, it was a stake-out."

"*You* were staking out the house?"

"Well, sure."

"But how did you know anyone would be there?"

"Well, it was just a strong feeling I had." Another strong feeling he had was that Cristabel didn't believe him.

"So what happened?"

"It's just like it said in the paper. These two guys tried to rob that bar with a phony gun. There was an off-duty cop there, and he pulled a real gun on them, but they got away. They ran like crazy. They didn't even have time to get back to the car they stole. They just made for the corridor. A squad car spotted them heading up Pepper Tree Street, but they disappeared before the cops could catch them."

Philo had a beauty of a story made up for Cristabel, all about how he had dealt single-handedly with the thugs and had cornered them for the police. Then he suddenly remembered how he felt about made-up stories. No, he couldn't do that to someone else. He said, "The paper was right. I *was* running away. But don't ask me why, because I don't want to talk about it."

She stared at him, a curious expression in her eyes, but said nothing.

Philo said, "I was hiding in that house when those guys came in and found me. And, man, was I scared! I was never so scared in my life. I thought they were going to kill me. Then Miss Jolly came. She remembered the house and took my dad there, and they found me." Philo smiled to himself, recalling how the headlights of his dad's VW had cast just enough light into the entry to make Miss Jolly look like a creature from outer space.

"The cops showed up because they wanted to know what my dad's car was doing there. After that, it was a cinch to catch those guys. They were really cornered in that boarded-up house."

"The paper said you all wound up in the police station."

"Yeah, we did. But they let Miss Jolly and me and my dad go right away. You see, my dad had already reported me missing, so all he had to do was explain about why he thought I might be in that house."

"Is that how they knew about the dogs?"

"Yeah. Miss Jolly told my dad and he told the cops, and, of course, the newspaper knew already."

Cristabel offered him another napoleon. This time he had to refuse. She said, "Well, anyhow, something good came out of it all. The paper said the dogs are cured now and there were enough donations to pay the vet bills and lots of people offered to give the dogs homes."

"Miss Jolly's keeping Princess Starlight. She always said she didn't want a dog because, at her age, the dog might outlive her. Then what would happen to the dog? It turns out Princess Starlight is an older dog. Miss Jolly says they'll just be two old ladies living out their lives together."

"Did she really say that?"

Philo nodded.

"Even if she *is* weird, that's beautiful. That is really beautiful."

"And guess who has Rajah?"

"I don't know."

"A friend of my dad's. Well, I guess I really

should say my dad's girlfriend. Her name's Marilyn. She said she'd take Rajah but only on one condition. I'd have to walk the dog every day after school. 'Course I was glad to help her out." Overjoyed was more like it. Rajah had readily given his stamp of approval to Marilyn, so Philo had to admit that there must be more good in the woman than immediately met the eye. Dogs were never wrong about those things.

Cristabel said, "That'll almost be like having a dog of your own."

"Yeah."

"You know, the Whipples said I could walk Mopey whenever I wanted to. Maybe we can walk the dogs together after school."

"Okay," Philo said agreeably.

At that point Todd and the other boys joined them at the table, and there was too much noise for conversation. Philo heard all sorts of remarks about his hat, but he was right. No matter what they said about it, it made them laugh. And when Cristabel gave them her remaining napoleons, the mood at the table was really festive.

When they all finished lunch, Cristabel whispered to Philo, "I've just got to tell you something important," so he hung behind the other boys to walk back to class with her.

Cristabel said, "The people who live on the other side of us have this perfectly adorable long-haired cat, Fluffy. She's not spayed, so she has kittens all the time, and these people just take them to the pound. I think that's awful, don't you?"

"Yeah," Philo said.

"From what my mother says, I preclude they want their kids to see how kittens are born. But what happens to those poor little kittens, I want to know?"

"Yeah," Philo said.

"People like that don't deserve a cat."

"Yeah," Philo said.

As they made their way toward the schoolroom, Cristabel went on, talking earnestly. After a time, Philo began shaking his head. Which could have indicated he was saying no to something or could have simply meant he was deploring the plight of those poor kittens. The wind had noisily set the pinwheel spinning atop Philo's beanie, so their voices were lost.

c.1

J
AME

Ames, Mildred.

Philo Potts, or, The
helping hand
strikes again

10.95

DATE			

© THE BAKER & TAYLOR CO.